THERE WERE SEVEN SUSPECTS

Kenneth Meer wasn't one of them. Yet a week after the explosion, he was in the psychiatric ward suffering from something the doctors called The Lady Macbeth Syndrome: **invisible blood on the hands.**

There were various possibilities: he had planted the bomb himself and the burden of guilt was too great for him. Or: he hadn't but knew who had. Or: the event itself was too heavy—the havoc, the shrapnel-shattered flesh, the blood on the walls . . .

All valid guesses. But just guesses. Meanwhile, a man who had killed for no reason was wandering around with a bomb in a briefcase.

This time he had all the reason in the world to kill . . . and kill again!

please pass the guilt

A NERO WOLFE NOVEL

rex stout

BANTAM BOOKS · TORONTO · LONDON · NEW YORK

PLEASE PASS THE GUILT

*A Bantam Book / published by arrangement with
The Viking Press, Inc.*

PRINTING HISTORY

Viking edition published September 1973
2nd printing ...... October 1973   3rd printing .... May 1974
Mystery Guild edition published September 1973

Bantam edition / October 1974
2nd printing .... October 1978

*Bantam Books are published by Bantam Books, Inc. Its trade-
mark, consisting of the words "Bantam Books" and the por-
trayal of a bantam, is registered in the United States Patent
Office and in other countries. Marca Registrada. Bantam
Books, Inc., 666 Fifth Avenue, New York, New York 10019.*

1

*h*e grunted—the low brief rumble that isn't meant to be heard—turned his head to dart a glance at me, and turned back to Dr. Vollmer, who was in the red leather chair facing the end of Wolfe's desk.

It wasn't just that he was being asked for a favor. It there was a man alive who could say no to a request for a favor easier than Nero Wolfe, I hadn't met him. The trouble was that it was Dr. Vollmer, whose house and office was only a few doors away, who had said he wanted one, and the favor score between him and us was close to a tie. So Wolfe was probably going to be stuck, and therefore the grunt.

Vollmer crossed his long, lean legs and rubbed his narrow, lean jaw with a knuckle. "It's really for a friend of mine," he said, "a man I would like to oblige. His name is Irwin Ostrow, a psychiatrist—not a Freudian. He's interested in a new approach to psychiatric therapy, and he's working at it. Crisis intervention, they call it. I'll have to explain how it works. It's based on—"

"First aid," Wolfe said. "Emotional tourniquet."

"How—you know about it?"

"I read. I read for various purposes, and one of them is to learn what my fellow beings are up

1

to. There are several thousand emergency-treatment centers now operating in this country. The Detroit Psychiatric Institute has a Suicide Prevention Center. The crisis center at Grady Memorial Hospital in Atlanta is staffed by psychiatrists, nurses, social workers, lay therapists, and clergymen. The director of clinical psychiatry at San Francisco General Hospital has written and spoken at length about it. His name is Decker."

"What's his first name?"

"Barry."

Vollmer shook his head. "You know," he said, "you are the most improbable combination of ignorance and knowledge on earth. You don't know what a linebacker does. You don't know what a fugue is."

"I try to know what I need to know. I make sure to know what I want to know."

"What if it's unknowable?"

"Only philosophers and fools waste time on the unknowable. I am neither. What does Dr. Ostrow want to know?"

Vollmer slid back in the red leather chair, which was deep. "Well. I don't want to bore you with things you already know. If I do, stop me. The Washington Heights Crisis Clinic is on 178th Street, near Broadway. It's a storefront operation; people can just walk in, and they do. A woman who can't stop beating her two-year-old daughter. A man who keeps getting up in the middle of the night and going outdoors in his pajamas. Most of them are on the way to a mental hospital if they're not headed off quick, and the clinic—but you know all that. Eight days ago, a week ago yesterday, a young man came and told a nurse he needed help and she sent him in to Irwin—Dr. Ostrow. He gave the nurse his name, Ronald Seaver."

Vollmer looked at me with his brows up. "I hope *they* don't have to go to a crisis clinic," I said, and turned to Wolfe. "One of your ignorance areas, baseball. Ron Swoboda is an outfielder and Tom Seaver is a pitcher. 'Ron Seaver' is obviously a phony, but it might help to know he's a Met fan, if a clue is needed."

"It is," Vollmer said. "Of course Irwin knew it was an alias, but people often do that their first visit. But he came back five days later, Saturday morning, and again the next day, Sunday, and he not only hasn't told his real name, he won't give any facts at all except what his crisis is. It's blood on his hands. His hands get covered with blood, not visible to anybody else, and he goes and washes them. The first time, ten days ago—no, twelve— it was in the middle of the night and he had to go to the bathroom and wash his hands. It happens any time, no pattern, day or night, but usually when he's alone. A nurse there says it's the Lady Macbeth syndrome. He says he knows of no event or experience that could have caused it, but Irwin is sure he's lying."

He turned a palm up. "So that's his crisis. Irwin says he really has one, a severe one; the possibility of a complete mental breakup is indicated. But they can't get through to him. One of Irwin's colleagues there is a woman, a lay therapist, who has had remarkable success with some tough ones, even catatonics, but after two hours with him—that was Sunday, day before yesterday —she told him he was wasting his time and theirs. Then she said she had alternative suggestions: either he could go to a surgeon and have his hands amputated, or he could go to a detective, perhaps Nero Wolfe, and try to dodge his questions. And do you know what he said? He said, 'I'll do that. I'll go to Nero Wolfe.' "

My brows were up. "He tried to," I said. "So that was Ron Seaver. He phoned yesterday around noon and said he wanted to come and pay Nero Wolfe a hundred dollars an hour to ask him questions. He wouldn't give his name and didn't mention bloody hands. Naturally I thought he was a nut and said no and hung up."

Vollmer nodded. "And he phoned Irwin and Irwin phoned me." To Wolfe: "Of course the hundred dollars an hour wouldn't tempt you, but I didn't come to tempt you, I came to ask a favor for a friend. You said you make sure to know what you want to know. Well, Dr. Ostrow thinks it's possible that this man *did* have blood on his hands, and he wants to know if he can and should be helped. I admit I do too. I've dealt with people in crises myself, any doctor has, but this is a new one to me."

Wolfe looked at the wall clock. Twenty minutes to seven. "Will you dine with us? Shad roe Creole. Fritz uses shallots instead of onion and no cayenne. Chablis, not sherry."

Vollmer smiled, broad. "Knowing how few people get invited to your table, I should beam. But I know it's only compassion for my—"

"I am *not* compassionate."

"Hah. You think my meals are like the one Johnson described to Boswell: 'ill-killed, ill-dressed, ill-cooked, and ill-served,' and you feel sorry for me. Thank you, but I have things to do before I eat. If I could come tomorrow and bring that man ..."

Wolfe made a face. "Not for dinner. I suppose he'll see Dr. Ostrow tomorrow, or telephone. If he does, tell him to come tomorrow evening at nine o'clock. There will be no fee. And no compassion."

t hat was Tuesday, the third of June. The next morning there was a little problem. When we haven't got a job or jobs going, I usually get out for a walk after breakfast, with or without an excuse like a trip to the bank, but that Wednesday I didn't. I don't know if I have ever mentioned that the three employees of the Midtown Home Service Corporation who come once a week are always male because Wolfe insists on it. That Wednesday Andy and Sam came at nine o'clock as usual, but they had a woman along, a husky coal-black female with shoulders nearly as broad as mine. Andy, who was white but broad-minded, explained that it was tougher than ever to get men, and repeated one of his favorite remarks, "Goddam it, TV men and carpet layers work in homes." He called the woman Lucile and started her on the dining room, across the hall from the office on the ground floor of the old brownstone. Of course Wolfe, up in the plant rooms on the roof for his morning session with the orchids, hadn't seen her. I went back to the kitchen, sat at my little breakfast table for my second cup of coffee, and told Fritz, "We'll tell him it's a man in disguise because he's wanted."

"There's batter for another cake, Archie."

"No, thanks. They're extra good, they always

are, but I've had five. He's wanted for peddling pot. Or maybe acid."

"But his front? The *monts?*"

"Part of the disguise. King-size bra. Is this the Brazilian coffee?"

"No, Colombian. Of course you're just talking. If he sees her—" He threw his hands, and aimed his eyes, up.

"But he probably will. He often comes to the kitchen while you're giving them lunch." I sipped hot coffee. "I'll tell him when he comes down. Have your ear plugs in, he may let out a roar."

So I didn't go for a walk. Anything could happen; Lucile might know about the orchids and sneak up for a look. I was at my desk in the office when the sound of the elevator came at eleven o'clock, and when Wolfe entered and told me good morning and went to put a cluster of Acampe pachyglossa in the vase on his desk, I said, "There's an amendment to the by-laws. Andy is here with Sam and a woman, a black one named Lucile. She is now up in your room with Andy. He says that more and more men think housework isn't manly, which is silly since Fritz and Theodore and I work in your house and we're as manly as they come. It looks like a case of circumstances beyond our control, but if you don't agree, control it."

He sat, got his nineteen stone (it looks better in stone than in pounds) arranged in his made-to-order chair, glanced at his desk calendar, and picked up the stack the mailman had brought. He looked at me. "Are there female Black Panthers?"

"I'll look it up. If there are, Lucile isn't one. She would be a black mare, Clydesdale or Percheron. She can pick up the vacuum cleaner with one finger."

"She is in my house by invitation. I'll have to speak with her, at least a nod and a word."

But he didn't. He didn't go to the kitchen

while they were there at lunch, and Andy, who knew Wolfe's habits, kept their paths from crossing. Their regular leaving time was four o'clock, but that was also the time for Wolfe's afternoon turn in the plant rooms, and Andy waited until he was in the elevator on his way up. With them gone, I relaxed. In view of Wolfe's basic attitude on women, there's no telling what will happen when one is in that house. I was making entries, from notes supplied by Theodore, on the germination and performance cards, when Dr. Vollmer phoned to say that Ronald Seaver would come at nine o'clock. The only preparation needed took about six minutes—going to a cabinet for a fancy glass-and-metal jar with the sharpened ends of a dozen pencils protruding at the top, and placing it at a certain spot and a certain angle near the right edge of my desk, and putting a certain plug in a certain hidden outlet.

He was nearly half an hour late. It was 9:23, and we had just finished with after-dinner coffee in the office, when the doorbell rang and I went. Going down the hall, what I saw on the stoop through the one-way glass panel was commonplace for anyone who knows midtown Manhattan: a junior executive, medium-sized, with a poorly designed face tired too young, in a dark gray suit that had been cut to fit, no hat. I opened the door and invited him in, and added as he entered, "If you had told me on the phone you were Ron Seaver I would have asked you to come and discuss the outlook."

He smiled—the kind of smile that comes quick and goes quicker—and mumbled, "They're doing better."

I agreed and ushered him down the hall. In the office, he stopped about three steps in and one foot backed up a little. I thought that at sight of Wolfe he was deciding to call it off, and so did he, but when I indicated the red leather chair, he

7

came to Wolfe's desk, muttered something, and put out a hand, and Wolfe said, "No, there's blood on it. Sit down."

He went to the red leather chair, sat, met Wolfe's eyes, and said, "If you could see it, if *you* could actually *see* it."

As I went to my chair at my desk I glanced at the jar of pencils; it was in position.

Wolfe nodded. "But I can't. If Dr. Vollmer has described the situation accurately it must be assumed that you are either obtuse or deranged. In your right mind, if you have one, you couldn't possibly expect the people at the clinic to help you unless you supplied some facts. Are you going to tell me your name?"

"No." It wasn't a mumble.

"Are you going to tell me anything at all? Where you live, where you work, where you have seen blood that other people saw or could have seen?"

"No." His jaw worked a little. "I explained to Dr. Ostrow that I couldn't. I knew that that clinic had done some remarkable things for people. I had been—I had heard about it. I thought it was just possible—I thought it was worth trying."

Wolfe turned to me. "How much did his suit cost?"

"Two hundred or more. Probably more. The shoes, at least forty."

"How much would a magazine or newspaper pay him for an article about that clinic?"

"My god," Ronald Seaver blurted, "that's not —" He bit it off and clamped his jaw.

"It's merely one of the valid conjectures." Wolfe shook his head. "I don't like to be imposed on, and I doubt if Dr. Ostrow does. The simplest way to learn if you are an impostor is to discover who and what you are. For Mr. Goodwin to follow you when you leave would take time and trouble, and it isn't necessary. —Archie?"

I picked up the jar and told Ronald Seaver, "Candid camera inside." I removed a couple of the pencils and held them up; they were only two-inch stubs. "Leaving room for the camera below. It now has eight shots of you. Tomorrow I'll show them to people I know—a newspaper man, a couple of cops—"

When you are sitting in a chair and a man comes at you, your reaction depends on what he has in mind. If he has an idea of hurting you, with or without a weapon, you get on your feet fast. But if he merely intends to take something from you, for instance a jar of pencils, and if you have decided that you are stronger and quicker than he is, you merely pull your feet back. Actually he didn't even come close. He stopped three steps short, turned to Wolfe, and said, "You can't do that. Dr. Ostrow wouldn't permit it."

Wolfe nodded. "Of course he wouldn't, but this office is not in his jurisdiction. You have presumed to take an evening of my time, and I want to know why. Are you desperately in need of help, or are you playing some silly game? I'll soon know, probably tomorrow, depending on how long it takes Mr. Goodwin to get you identified from the photographs. I hope it won't be prolonged; I am merely doing a favor for a friend. Good evening, sir. I'll communicate with Dr. Ostrow, not with you."

With me it had been a tossup whether the guy was in some kind of bad jam or was merely on a complicated caper. His long, pointed nose, which didn't go well with his wide, square chin, had twitched a couple of times, but that didn't prove anything. Now, however, he gave evidence. His half-closed, unblinking eyes, steady at me, with a deep crease across his forehead, showed that something was really hurting.

"I don't believe it," he said louder than necessary, since he was only two arm's lengths away.

Without letting my eyes leave him, I reached for the jar, which I had put back on my desk, stood, removed the top that held the pencil stubs, tilted the jar to show him what was inside, and said, "Autophoton, made in Japan. Electronic control. One will get you ten I'll have you tagged by sundown tomorrow."

His lips parted to let words out, but none came. His head turned to Wolfe, then back to me, and then he turned clear around and took a slow, short step, and another, and I thought he was heading out. But he veered to the right, toward the big globe near the book shelves, stopped halfway to it, and stood. Apparently he wanted his face to himself while he decided something. It took him a good two minutes, maybe three. He turned, got a leather case from his breast pocket, took things from it, selected one—a card—went to Wolfe's desk, and handed it to him. By the time Wolfe had given it a look, I was there, and he passed it to me. It was a New York driver's license: Kenneth Meer, 5 feet 11, age 32, 147 Clover Street, New York 10012.

"Saving you the trouble of asking questions," he said, and extended a hand. I gave him the card and he put it back in the case and the case in his pocket; and he turned and went. Not slow short steps; he marched. I followed out to the hall, and when he had opened the front door and crossed the sill and pulled the door shut, not banging it, I went back to my desk, sat, cocked my head at Wolfe, and spoke:

"You told Doc Vollmer yesterday that you read to learn what your fellow beings are up to. Well?"

He scowled. "I have told you a dozen times that 'Doc' is an obnoxious vulgarism."

"I keep forgetting."

"Pfui. You never forget anything. It was deliberate. As for Kenneth Meer, there has been no picture of him in the *Times*. Has there been one in the *Gazette?*"

"No. His name several times, but no picture. Nor any report that he got blood on his hands, but of course he saw plenty. I suppose, since it's a favor for a friend, I'll have to see a couple of people and find out—"

"No. Get Dr. Vollmer."

"But shouldn't I—"

"No."

I swiveled and swung the phone around. Of Vollmer's three numbers, the most likely one at that hour was the unlisted one on the third floor of his house, and when I dialed it he answered himself. Wolfe got at his phone and I stayed on.

"Good evening, doctor. That man came, half an hour late, and has just left. He refused to give us any information, even his name, and we had to coerce him by a ruse with a concealed camera. Under constraint he identified himself by showing us his motor vehicle operator's license, and then departed without a word. His name has recently been in the news in connection with a murder, but only as one of those present at the scene; there has been no published indication that he is under suspicion or is likely to be. Do you want his name, for Dr. Ostrow?"

"Well." Silence for at least ten seconds. "You got it by—uh—coercion?"

"Yes. As I said."

"Then I don't think—" Another silence, shorter. "I doubt if Irwin would want it. He never uses coercion. May I ask him and let you know?"

"Certainly."

"Do you intend— Are you interested in the murder? Professionally?"

"Only as a spectator. I am not involved and don't expect to be."

Vollmer thanked him for the favor, not enthusiastically, and they hung up. Wolfe looked at

11

the wall clock—five past ten—and reached for his current book, *Grant Takes Command,* by Bruce Catton. I went to the hall and up the two flights to my room, to catch the last inning or two at Shea Stadium on television.

3

We keep both the *Times* and the *Gazette* for three weeks, sometimes longer, and even if the bank balance had been at a record high I would probably have had another go at the accounts of the Odell murder just for curiosity, since I had now met one of the cast of characters. But we needed a job. In the past five months, the first five of 1969, we had had only six cases, and the fee had gone to five figures in only one of them—getting a damn fool out of a nasty mess with a bunch of smoothies he should have been on to at the first contact. So the checking account balance had lost a lot of weight, and to meet the upkeep of the old brownstone, including the weekly payroll for Theodore and Fritz and me, by about the middle of July Wolfe would have to turn some documents into cash, and that should be prevented if possible. So it wasn't just curiosity that sent me to the basement Thursday morning for old newspapers.

The murder was two weeks old, but what had happened, and how, had been plain and clear in the first reports and had not been substantially revised or amended. At 3:17 P.M. on Tuesday, May 20, a man named Peter J. Odell had entered a room on the sixth floor of the CAN building on West Fifty-fourth Street, pulled open the bottom drawer of a desk, and died instantly. The bomb that shredded him was so powerful that it not only blew the metal desk up to the ceiling but even buckled two of the walls. CAN stood for Continental Air Network, which occupied the whole building, and Peter J. Odell had been its vice-president in charge of development. The room and desk were not his; they belonged to Amory Browning, the vice-president in charge of programming.

All right, that was what happened, but in addition to the main question, who had put the bomb in the drawer, there were others that had still not been answered, at least not for publication. It wasn't unheard of for a vice-president to enter another vice-president's room, but why had Odell opened that drawer? *That* drawer. It was known to enough people at CAN to get into both the *Times* and the *Gazette* that that drawer had rarely, possibly never, been opened by anyone but Browning himself because nothing was kept in it but a bottle or bottles of twelve-year-old Ten-Mile Creek bourbon. It had almost certainly been known to Odell.

No one had admitted seeing Odell enter Browning's room. Helen Lugos, Browning's secretary, whose room adjoined his, had been down the hall in a file room. Kenneth Meer, Browning's chief assistant, had been down on the ground floor in conference with some technicians. Browning himself had been with Cass R. Abbott, the president of CAN, in his office—the corner office on that floor. If anyone knew why Odell had gone to Browning's room, he wasn't saying. So the answer to the question, Who put the bomb in the drawer? depended partly on the answer to another question: Whom did he expect to open the drawer?

Rereading the accounts in fifteen copies of the *Times* and fifteen of the *Gazette*, I was impressed by how well I had absorbed the details of an event we had not been involved in, and by nothing else. There was nothing to give me a nudge on a start of what I had in mind. It was after eleven o'clock when I finished, so Wolfe had come down from the plant rooms, and I went up to the phone in my room to dial a number—the switchboard of the *Gazette*. It was an afternoon paper and Lon Cohen's line was usually busy from 10 A.M. to 4:20 P.M., but I finally got him. I told him I wanted thirty seconds and he said I could have five.

"Then," I said, "I won't tell you about the steer that grew the Chateaubriands that Felix is saving for us. Can you meet me at Rusterman's at a quarter past six?"

"I can if I have to. Bringing what?"

"Just your tongue. And of course plenty of lettuce for later."

The "later" meant the poker game at Saul Panzer's apartment which started at eight o'clock Thursday evenings. Lon made an appropriate retort about lettuce and hung up, and I dialed another number I didn't have to look up and got Felix, and told him that this time my request for the small room upstairs was strictly personal, not on behalf of Wolfe, and that if he was short on Chateaubriands, tournedos would be fine. He asked what kind of flowers would be preferred, and I said my guest would be a man from whom I hoped to get some useful information, so instead of flowers make it four-leaf clovers for luck.

An announcement to Wolfe that I wouldn't be there for dinner was not required, since I never was on Thursdays. Since his dinner time was 7:15, I couldn't eat at his table and be at Saul's poker table at eight. I merely mentioned casually, after we had finished with the morning mail, that I would be leaving around a quarter to six, before he came down from the plant rooms. I did not mention Kenneth Meer, and neither did he, but around the middle of the afternoon Vollmer phoned to say that Dr. Ostrow didn't want to know what Ronald Seaver's name was. Which of course

15

was a polite lie. Dr. Ostrow would certainly have liked to know the name, but not from Wolfe if he had got it by a trick.

The small room upstairs at Rusterman's had many memories for me, back to the days when Marko Vukcic was still alive and making it the best restaurant in New York, with frequent meals with his old friend Nero Wolfe helping to keep it the best. It was still better than good, as Lon Cohen remarked that evening after his third spoonful of Germiny à l'Oseille, and again after his second bite of Chateaubriand and his first sip of the claret.

With about his fourth sip he said, "I'd be enjoying this more—or less, I don't know which— if I knew the price. Of course you want something, or Nero Wolfe does. What?"

I swallowed meat. "Not Nero Wolfe. Me. He doesn't know about it and I don't want him to. I need some facts. I spent two hours this morning reading everything two great newspapers have printed about the murder of Peter J. Odell and I still don't know enough for my personal satisfaction. I thought a chat with you might be helpful."

He squinted at me. "How straight is that? That Wolfe doesn't know you're feeding me."

"As straight as from a ten to an ace."

His eyes aimed about a foot above my head, as they often did when he was deciding whether to call or raise, stayed there while I buttered a bite of roll, and leveled down to mine. "Well, well," he said. "You could just put an ad in the *Gazette*. Of course with a box number since Wolfe mustn't know you're drumming."

Just looking at Lon you would never guess, from his neat little face and his slick black hair, how sharp he is. But people who know him know, including the publisher of the *Gazette*, which is why he has a room to himself two doors down the hall from the publisher's room.

I shook my head. "The kind of people I want to reach don't read *Gazette* ads. To be perfectly frank, I'm going stale and I need exercise. There must be plenty about that crowd that isn't fit to print. This room isn't bugged and neither am I. Have Cramer and the DA got a lead that they're saving?"

"No." He forked peas. "Almost certainly not. Of course the hitch is that they don't know who the bomb was intended for." He put the peas where he wanted them. "Probably no one does but the guy who planted it. It's reasonable to suppose it was meant for Browning, but after all it was Odell who got it. A fact is a fact. Did Browning plant it *for* Odell? He did have a motive."

"Good enough?"

"Apparently. Of course you know that Abbott is retiring the last of August and the board of directors was going to decide on his successor at a meeting scheduled for five o'clock that afternoon, and it would be either Browning or Odell. Odell certainly didn't plant the bomb for Browning and then open the drawer himself, but did Browning plant it and somehow get Odell to open it?"

I sipped claret. "Of course your best men are on it, or have been. What do they think?"

"They've quit thinking. All they have is guesses. Landry's guess is that Mrs. Browning put the bomb there for Helen Lugos, her husband's secretary, knowing, or thinking she knew, that Helen checked the bourbon supply every morning."

"Did she? Check the bourbon supply every morning?"

"I don't know and I doubt if Cramer does. Helen isn't speaking to reporters and it is said that she isn't wasting any words with the law. Also I don't know for sure that Helen and Browning were bedding, but Landry thinks he does. Ask Inspector Cramer, he may know. Another guess,

17

Gahagan's, is that Odell was setting the bomb for Browning and fumbled it. He has been trying for a week to trace where and how Odell got the bomb. Perlman's guess is that Abbott did it because he thought they were going to pick Browning for the new president and he was for Odell. He has three theories on why Odell went to Browning's room and opened the drawer, none of them much good. Damiano's guess is that Helen Lugos did it, to get Browning, but he is no better than Perlman on why Odell horned in."

"Why would Helen want to get Browning?"

"Sex."

"That's not responsive."

"Certainly it's responsive. When sex comes in by the window, logic leaves by the door. When two people collaborate sexually, either one is capable of doing anything and nobody can be sure he knows why he did it. I think Damiano's guess is based on something a man named Meer, Kenneth Meer, told him. Meer is Browning's chief of staff. Damiano got him talking the day after it happened—they had been choir boys together at St. Andrew's—and Meer said that anyone who wanted to know how it happened should concentrate on Helen Lugos. Of course Damiano kept at him then, but Meer backed off. And as I said, Helen isn't doing any talking."

"Has Damiano told Inspector Cramer what Meer said?"

"Of course not. He didn't even tell us until a couple of days ago. He was hoping to earn a medal."

"Does anybody guess that Meer did it?"

"No one at the *Gazette* does. Naturally he has been considered, everybody has, but even for a wild guess you've got to have a motive. Meer certainly wouldn't have wanted to get Browning; if Browning is made president, Meer will be right up near the top. And how could he have got Odell to go to Browning's room and open that drawer? Of course guesses are a dime a dozen. If the bomb was intended for Browning, there are at least a dozen possible candidates. For instance, Madeline Odell, now the widow Odell. She had been expecting her husband to be the CAN president ever since she married him, twenty years ago, and it looked as if Browning was going to get it instead. Or Theodore Falk, the Wall Street Falk, old friend of the Odells and a member of the CAN board of directors. Of course he didn't do it himself, but millionaires don't have to do things themselves. Or Sylvia Venner. You know?"

I nodded. " 'The Big Town.' "

"Right. She had that program for two years and Browning bounced her. Now she does chores, and she hates Browning's guts. I could name more. Of course if the bomb was intended for Odell, there are candidates for that too, but for them there's the problem of getting Odell to enter that room and open that drawer."

I swallowed my last bite of Chateaubriand and pushed the button for Pierre. "You said Odell's wife had been expecting him to be president ever since she married him. Had she been doing anything about it?"

"Plenty. She inherited a big block of CAN stock from her father, Carl Hartig, along with a lot of oil wells and miscellaneous items, and she's been on the board of directors for ten years. She would probably have given half of her seventy or eighty million to have Browning removed from competition, but if she had known that bomb was in that drawer she would have made damn sure that her husband wouldn't go near that room that day. That's why she's not *my* guess—or anybody else's as far as I know."

"Seventy or eighty *million?*"

19

"At least that. She's really loaded."

"Huh. What kind of sauce do you want on your soufflé? Brandy ginger or mocha rum?"

"Mocha rum sounds better."

Pierre had come and was removing empty dishes. I told him what we would have and waited until he was gone to resume with Lon. You never know. Abbott or Browning or Madeline Odell might be one of Pierre's pet customers.

When, at a quarter to eight, out on the sidewalk, we decided to walk the eleven blocks to Saul Panzer's instead of scouting for a taxi, I had collected around a hundred more facts and guesses, but it would be a waste of paper and ink to list them for you since none of them was any help to my program. Also I will not report on the course of events at the poker table, except to say that having a complicated operation on my mind was no help to my wallet. I lost sixty-eight bucks.

4

*t*he first problem was how to get to her, and the
second one was what to say when I did. "Her" was
of course Madeline Odell, the widow. She was almost certainly in the clear on the bomb, she had the
best reason for wanting the bomber to be caught
and nailed, and she had the biggest stack. It was
those two problems trying to take over that had
caused me to make three big mistakes and several
small ones at the poker game, and cost me money.
They did not keep me from getting a good eight
hours' sleep, nothing ever does, and they didn't
affect my appetite at breakfast, but I skipped
things in the *Times* that I usually cover, and I
guess I was short with Fritz. In the office I actually forgot to put fresh water in the vase on
Wolfe's desk.

I still hadn't decided at lunchtime. Of course
any one of a dozen dodges would have got me to
her; no one is inaccessible if you put your mind on
it; but then what? If possible the approach should
lead naturally to the proposition. After lunch I
went for a walk with a couple of unnecessary
errands for an excuse, and didn't get back until
after four o'clock, so Wolfe was up in the plant
rooms and I had the office to myself. I swung the
typewriter around and rolled paper in and gave it
a try.

Dear Mrs. Odell: This is on Nero Wolfe's letterhead because I work for him and am writing it in his office, but it is strictly personal, from me, and Mr. Wolfe doesn't know I am writing you. I do so because I am an experienced professional detective and it hurts me to see or read about poor detective work, especially in an important case like the murder of your husband. Mr. Wolfe and I have of course followed the published accounts of the investigation, and yesterday he remarked to me that apparently the most crucial fact was being ignored, or at least not getting the priority it deserved, and I agreed with him. Such a criticism from him to the police or the District Attorney would probably have no effect, but it occurred to me this morning that it might have some effect if it came from you. If you wish to reach me the address and telephone number are above.

I read it over twice and made five improvements: I took out "strictly" and "professional," changed "poor" to "inferior," "crucial" to "important," and "priority" to "attention." I read it again, changed "an important case like" to "such a vital case as," typed it on a letterhead with two carbons, signed it, and addressed an envelope to a number on East Sixty-third Street. I went to the kitchen to tell Fritz I was going out for air, and walked to the post office on Eighth Avenue.

Since it was a Friday afternoon in June, it was possible, even probable, that she wouldn't get it until Monday, and nothing would interfere with my weekend pleasures at Shea Stadium, but a little after eleven o'clock Saturday morning, when Wolfe was dictating a long letter to an orchid collector in Malaysia, the phone rang and I swiveled and took it.

"Nero Wolfe's office, Archie Goodwin speaking."

A businesslike female voice: "This is Mrs. Peter Odell's secretary. She has received your letter and wishes to speak to Mr. Wolfe."

Of course I had known that might happen, with Wolfe right there. "I'm sorry," I said, "but Mr. Wolfe isn't available and won't be until Monday. Anyway I made it clear that the letter was personal."

She covered the transmitter and I heard nothing. In a couple of minutes she was back: "Mr. Goodwin?"

"Here."

"Mrs. Odell wishes to see you. Will you be here promptly at three o'clock?"

One of my basic opinions is that people who take things for granted should be helped to a better understanding of democracy, and at three o'clock it would be about the fourth inning, but I hadn't been asked to write that letter. "Yes," I said, "I'll be there," and hung up, and swiveled.

"Someone using your name in vain," I told Wolfe. "People should read letters at least three times." I looked at my notebook. "The last I have is 'in spite of all the crosses hybridizers have tried.' "

It took another full page of the notebook.

My intention had been to get to Shea Stadium a little after one and enjoy a couple of hot dogs and a pint of milk while watching batting practice. Instead, I got to Sam's diner on Tenth Avenue a little after one and enjoyed rye bread and baked beans, two items that never appear at Wolfe's table, and then walked the nearly two miles from West Thirty-fifth Street to East Sixty-third. The people you see on midtown sidewalks Saturday afternoons are completely different from other days.

It was a five-story, forty-foot-wide stone mansion, between Fifth and Madison, and I was stopped at the entrance to the vestibule by a broad-shouldered husky with a Lathrop Protective Service badge on his buttoned-up jacket. Apparently after more than two weeks, pests—for instance, journalists—were still a problem, or Mrs. Odell thought they were. He said grimly, "Well, sir?"

I pronounced my name and said I was expected, and produced evidence of my identity from my card case. He entered the vestibule and pushed the button, and the door was opened by a woman in a neat gray uniform with a skirt that reached a good four inches below her knees who accepted my name without evidence. She crossed the marble floor to an intercom on a marble table and told it Mr. Goodwin was there, and in a couple of minutes there was the sound of an elevator about one-tenth as noisy as Wolfe's. A door at the far end of the large entrance hall slid open, and a woman stuck her head out and invited me to join her. We went up past two doors and stopped at the third, and she led me down the hall to an open door at the front and stood aside for me to enter.

It was a big room, the whole width of the house, and my sweeping glance saw desks, working chairs and easy chairs, two couches, oil paintings, filing cabinets, a color television—and my glance stopped there because a ball game was on, Ralph Kiner was talking, and his audience was a woman propped against a bank of cushions on an oversized couch. Even if it hadn't been her house I would have recognized her from her pictures in the *Times* and *Gazette:* a face bulged in the middle by wide cheek bones, and a wide full-lipped mouth. Her loose, pale blue dress or robe or sack was zippered shut in front, top to bottom. I crossed over to her and asked politely, "What's the score?"

Her brown eyes darted to me and back to the game. "Mets two, Pirates four, last of the fourth. Sit down."

I went to a chair not far from the couch that faced the TV set. Ed Kranepool was at bat. He went to three and two and then grounded out, ending the inning, and a commercial started yapping. As I looked around for the secretary and saw she wasn't there, the sound quit and I turned back to Mrs. Odell. Remote control; she had pushed a button.

"I'll leave the picture on," she said. She sized me up head to foot, taking her time. My pants were pressed. "That was a poor excuse for a letter you sent me. 'The most important fact,' you said, but you didn't say what it is."

"Of course I didn't."

"Why 'of course'?"

The commercial had finished and a Pirate was coming to bat. She left the sound off but sent her eyes back to the game, so I sent mine, too. "I work for Nero Wolfe," I told the Pirate as he swung and missed. "He makes a living solving problems for people, and part of what they pay him pays my salary. It would be pretty dumb for me to tell people for free what he has said about their problems. I wrote that letter only because I hate to see a case bobbled."

"Oh, come off it." Her eyes darted to me and back to the game. "You invited me to reach you and wouldn't put him on when I phoned. How much do you want?"

"You might try a million. No one has ever bid high enough to make it tough for me. But I did invite you to reach me, didn't I? Do you know what I suspect? I'll bet that at the back of my mind, down in the subconscious, there was a sneaking idea that after two weeks and three days of the cops and the DA getting nowhere, you

25

might want to discuss it with Nero Wolfe. Do you know anything about him?"

"Personally and definitely, no. I know his reputation, certainly."

One Pirate had watched a third strike go by and another one had popped up to the infield. Now a third one lofted a major-league blooper out to left center and both Cleon Jones and Tommy Agee were on the gallop. It would fall in . . . but it didn't. Jones stretched an arm and one-handed it, and kept it. A good inning for Koosman. As the picture of the commercial started, I turned to the couch. "To be honest," I said, "I may as well admit that that letter *was* dumb. How could you needle the police or the District Attorney about neglecting the most important fact if I didn't tell you what it is? I apologize, and I not only apologize, I pay a forfeit. The most important fact is that your husband entered that room and opened that drawer, and the most important question is, why? Unless and until they have the answer to that the ten best investigators in the world couldn't possibly solve the case. Tell Inspector Cramer that, but don't mention Nero Wolfe. The sound of that name riles him." I stood up. "I realize that it's possible that you know why he entered the room and opened the drawer, and you have told the DA and he's saving it, but from the published accounts I doubt it, and so does Mr. Wolfe. Thank you for letting me see Cleon Jones make that catch."

I turned and was going, but she raised her voice. "Damn it, sit down!"

I did so, and as I sat Jerry Grote lined a double to the right-field corner. Bud Harrelson beat out a bunt and Grote moved to third, and Mrs. Odell pushed the button and the sound came on. More action and two Mets crossed the plate. When Ed Charles made the third out the score was tied, and as the commercial started she pushed the button, looked at me, and said, "Call Wolfe and tell him I want to see him. Now." She aimed a finger. "The phone on that desk. How long will it take him?"

"Too long. Forever. You certainly don't know him 'definitely.' He leaves his house only for personal errands no one else can do, never on business. I suppose you'd rather not discuss it on the phone, so you'll have to go to him. The address is on the letterhead. Six o'clock would be a good time, he'll be available then, and the game will be—"

"My god, what a nerve," she said. "You think I would?"

"No, I think you wouldn't. But you said you want to see him, and I—"

"All right, all right. Forget it." She pushed the button. Bob Murphy had replaced Ralph Kiner and he talks louder. She had to raise her voice: "Miss Haber will take you down. She's in the hall."

I got up and went. I hadn't the slightest idea, as I was escorted to the elevator and down, and to the entrance, by Miss Haber, and as I walked to Madison Avenue and turned downtown, headed for a bar where I knew there was a TV, whether or not I had wasted a letterhead and a postage stamp and most of an afternoon. On a bet I would have taken either end. But after all, she had said she wanted to see him, and if I know women one-tenth as well as Wolfe pretends to think I do, she was strongly inclined to get what she wanted. By the time the game ended, which the Mets won 7 to 5, I would no longer have taken either end. Two to one I had hooked her. That was how it looked as I used my key on the door of the old brownstone a little before six o'clock.

Of course I couldn't leave the house that evening. When I'm not there Fritz usually answers the phone, but sometimes Wolfe does, and she might call any minute. She *might*. She didn't. It was also possible that she would tell either Cramer or the DA about it and he would call. He didn't. When I went to bed around midnight the odds were no longer two to one. But there was still an off chance, and when I went to the office after breakfast Sunday morning, I rang Lily Rowan and told her I was stuck for the day and would send the tickets for the ball game by messenger, and I hoped she could find someone who could yell at the umpire as loud as I did. And then, about eight minutes after the messenger had come and taken the tickets, the phone rang, and it was Mrs. Odell in person, not the secretary. She said she wanted to speak with Wolfe and I said no, that he didn't even know I had written her and seen her.

"My god," she said, "you might think he's the President. I want to see him. Bring him."

"'I can't and he wouldn't. Honestly, Mrs. Odell, I wish he would. It would do him good to get out more, but not a chance. If there was a way of scoring pigheadedness it would be interesting to match him with you. I think he'd win."

"Of course I'm pigheaded. I always have been."

"I'm perfectly willing to make it 'strong-minded' if you prefer."

Silence. It lasted so long that I thought she had quit without bothering to hang up. Then she said, "I'll be there at six o'clock."

"Today? Sunday?"

"Yes." She hung up.

I took a deep breath and enjoyed it. So far so good, but the highest hurdle was still ahead. The Sunday household routine was different. Theodore didn't come on Sunday and Wolfe's morning with the orchids could be anything from twenty minutes to four hours. Also Fritz might leave for the day right after breakfast, or he might not. That day not, he had said. The question was when to spring it. Going up to the plant rooms with it was of course out of the question; I wasn't welcome there even for a real emergency. I decided not to decide until he came down and I saw what his mood was like.

When he showed, a little after eleven, he had the Sunday *Times* under one arm and a fourteen-inch raceme of Peristeria elata in the other hand, and his "Good morning" was a greeting, not just a growl. So when the flowers were in the vase and his bulk was satisfactorily arranged in the made-to-order chair he wouldn't swap for its weight in uranium, I spoke.

"Before you get started on the *Review of the Week*, I have an item you won't like. A woman is coming to see you at six o'clock today. Mrs. Peter J. Odell, whose husband opened a desk drawer and died. I had to ignore the rule on consulting you before making an appointment."

He was glaring at me. "I was here. I was available."

"Sure, but it was an emergency." I opened a drawer of my desk and took out a paper. "This is a carbon of a letter I sent her Friday afternoon." I rose, handed it to him, and returned to my chair. "She phoned yesterday morning, or her secretary did, and I went to see her yesterday afternoon, at her house on Sixty-third Street. She asked me to phone you to come, which of course wasn't discussable. I told her the only place she could see you was your office. She phoned this morning, an hour ago, and said she would be here at six o'clock.

He had read the letter. He read it again, with his lips pressed tight. He dropped it on his desk and looked at me. Not a glare or a scowl, just a hard, straight look. "I don't believe it," he said. "It would be insufferable, as you well know."

I nodded. "Of course that's the reaction I expected. But she'll be here at six. The emergency I referred to is in the safe. Your checkbook. You have of course noticed that since May first I have been giving you a memo of the condition every week instead of twice a month. Of the hundred and fifty-eight days this year you have worked about ten and I have worked less than twenty, not counting office chores. I happened—"

"Not 'less' than twenty. 'Fewer.' "

"Thank you. I happened to learn that Mrs. Odell's pile goes to eight figures, maybe even nine. The alternatives were (a) quit this job and make her an offer, or (b) get her to make you an offer. I tossed a coin and you won. So I wrote her that letter."

"Now," he said through his teeth with his lips barely moving, "*I* have alternatives."

"Certainly. Fire me, or go to work. If you fire me I won't expect severance pay. I would have to draw the check, and for more than a month every time I have drawn a check I have had to set my jaw. In deciding, please remember that at least twice you have yourself put out a hook when the bank balance got too low for comfort. The last time was when you sent me to see a woman named Fraser. The only difference is that this time I did it without consulting you. I like to earn *part* of my pay."

He cupped his hands over the ends of the chair arms, leaned back, and shut his eyes. But his lips didn't start to work in and out, so he didn't really have a problem; he was just looking at it. He may have thought I was holding my breath, but probably not, because he knows me nearly as well as I know him.

I was about to swivel and resume with my copy of the *Times* when he opened his eyes and straightened up and spoke. "Regarding my remark to you about the most important fact that is not getting the attention it deserves. She will of course want to know what it is, and so do I. Have you a suggestion?"

"Sure. I have already told her, yesterday. It's that Odell entered Browning's room and opened the drawer of his desk that everybody knew had only bourbon in it. Why? That's the most important question. You have only read the newspaper accounts, but I have also discussed it for an hour and a half with Lon Cohen and learned a few things that haven't been printed."

"Confound it." He made a face. "Very well. Talk. From Mr. Cohen, the substance. Your conversation with that woman, verbatim."

I talked.

5

*M*ost of the people who enter that office for the first time have something eating them, but even so they often notice one or more of the objects in view—the fourteen-by-twenty-six Keraghan rug or the three-foot globe or the floral display in the vase on Wolfe's desk. Mrs. Peter J. Odell didn't. When I escorted her to the office, her eyes fixed on Wolfe and stayed there as she crossed the rug and stopped just short of his desk. Of course he stayed put in his chair, as usual.

"Charlotte Haber is my secretary," she said. "I have brought her because I may need her." She went to the red leather chair, sat, and put her handbag on the little stand at her elbow. Meanwhile I had moved up one of the yellow chairs for the secretary. From the look Miss Haber had given me at the door, and the one she was now giving Wolfe, it was a good guess that she would rather have been somewhere else. The crease in her narrow forehead made it even narrower, and the way she was puckering her mouth, which was too small anyway, made it almost invisible.

"I have asked three men about you," Mrs. Odell told Wolfe. "You're highhanded and opinionated, and you charge high fees, but you're dependable."

Wolfe grunted. "You should have inquired further. Competence?"

"Oh, apparently you're smart enough. I'll decide that myself. Your man told me that you said the police are neglecting the most important question, why did my husband go to Browning's room and open that drawer? I want to know why that is so important." She got her bag and opened it and took out a checkfold. "How much for telling me that?"

He shook his head. "I discuss details only with clients and you haven't hired me. But since Mr. Goodwin has presumed to quote me to you— without my prior knowledge—I'll make an exception. On trial for murder, a man may be convicted without proof of motive. Establishment of motive of course helps with a jury, but it is not requisite. But in an *investigation* of a murder, motive is of first importance. The question was first asked in an ancient language many centuries ago: *Cui bono?* To try to learn who put that bomb in that drawer without knowing whom it was intended for is close to hopeless, and to learn whom it was intended for it is essential to know why your husband entered the room and opened the drawer, and who knew he was going to. Actually that's the most important question: Who knew he was going to? Did anybody? If it were my problem I would begin by concentrating on that question to the exclusion of all others. I give you that, madam, with my compliments, since Mr. Goodwin quoted me without bothering to get permission."

She still had the checkfold in her hand. "The police think it was intended for Amory Browning."

"No doubt. A reasonable assumption. But if it was actually intended for your husband, they're wasting their time and they'll get nowhere."

"Why do you think it was intended for my husband?"

"I don't. But I think it might have been—and I repeat, I would want first to learn if anyone knew he was going to enter that room and open that drawer, and if so, who."

She sat and looked at him. Then she turned her head to look at me, and turned it further to look at Charlotte Haber. I don't know if that was any help, but probably she had already made up her mind and didn't even know she was doing it. She opened the checkfold, slid a pen out of its loop, wrote, on both the stub and the check, and tore the check out. "You said I haven't hired you," she said. "Now I have. This twenty thousand dollars is for a retainer. I'm going to tell you something and ask you what to do, with the understanding that it is in confidence and you will never tell anyone about it—under any circumstances."

Wolfe shook his head. "I can't accept it on those terms."

"My god, why not? A lawyer would."

"I am not a member of the bar. What a client tells me is not a privileged communication. Archie. Your notebook."

I got it from a drawer, and a pen.

"One carbon," he said. "I acknowledge receipt of a check for twenty thousand dollars from Mrs. Peter J. Odell as a retainer for my services. Period. I guarantee that any information she gives me will be revealed to no one, comma, either by me or by Archie Goodwin, comma, without her consent, comma, unless circumstances arise that put me or him under legal compulsion to reveal it." He turned to her. "I assure you that we do not invite or welcome legal compulsion. Will that do?"

"I don't—I'll look at it."

I put paper in the typewriter and hit the keys. On the wall back of my desk is a mirror four feet high and six feet wide, and in it I could see that Miss Haber was looking surprised. No female secretary thinks a man can use eight fingers and two thumbs on a typewriter. I rolled it out, kept the carbon, and got up to hand Wolfe the original. He signed it and handed it back, and I took it to Mrs. Odell. She read it, pursed her lips, read it again, folded it and put it in her bag, and handed me the check. I gave it a look and took it to Wolfe, and without even a glance at it he dropped it on his desk.

He looked at the client: "I signed that receipt, madam, but I shall not consider myself definitely committed until I learn what you want me to do. I hope it won't be necessary for me to return your check, but I can if I must. In any case, what you tell me will be held in confidence if possible. What do you want?"

"I want advice. I want to know what *I* can do. I know why my husband went to Amory Browning's room and opened that drawer. So does Miss Haber. That's why she's here. I know the bomb was intended for him, and I know who put it there."

I suppose Wolfe has been surprised by things people have said as often as you or me, but his ego has arranged with him not to show it and he rarely does. But that got him. His eyes stretched wide, as wide as I have ever seen them, then they narrowed at her, half closed, and he cleared his throat.

"Indeed," he said. "Have you told the police?"

"No. I have told no one. No one knows about it except Miss Haber and me. I have hoped the police would get him. Why haven't they found out where and how he got the bomb? My god, are they any good at all? It has been more than two weeks. Now, after what you have said, I have got to do something and I want you to tell me what. How much do you know? Do you know that there was to be a directors' meeting at five o'clock that day to decide who would be the new president of CAN?"

"Yes. And that it would be either your husband or Mr. Browning."

She nodded. "And they were both to be at the meeting, and give their ideas about policy and what they thought should be done, and answer questions, and then leave, and we would discuss it and then vote. Did you know that?"

"No."

"Well, that's how it was. If you have read the papers, you know that Amory Browning kept a certain brand of whisky in that bottom drawer of his desk."

"Yes."

"And that every afternoon around four o'clock he took a drink of it."

"That has been said, yes."

"Well, he did. Every afternoon, between four and five o'clock. Everybody knew it. All right, now I'm telling you what you have guaranteed not to repeat. My husband went to that room and opened that drawer to put something in the whisky. It was my idea. Do you know what LSD is?"

"Yes. Lysergic acid diethylamide."

"My god, you can pronounce it. Well, I got some. You don't need to know how I got it. Miss Haber knows. I got some, it was a powder, and I put it in a little plastic container, and I persuaded my husband to use it. The police know he had it. It was in a pocket of his jacket. You didn't know about *that*."

"No."

"They haven't told about it. I think they haven't told anyone but me, and I told them I knew nothing about it. He was going to put it in the whisky. Almost certainly Browning would take a drink before he went to that meeting at five o'clock. We didn't know what that amount of LSD would do to him—of course we didn't know how full the bottle would be. But there was a good chance it would do enough for him to make a bad impression at that meeting, and it was understood and agreed that we would make a final decision that day. All right, now you know why he went to that room and opened that drawer."

Wolfe nodded. "I probably do. It isn't likely that you would trump up a tale of such an exploit —and the police have the LSD. You said that Miss Haber knows how you got it. Did she also know how you planned to use it?"

"Yes."

"Did anyone else know?"

"Yes. Amory Browning."

Wolfe shook his head. "My credulity will stretch only so far, madam. Obviously you are going to tell me that Mr. Browning murdered your husband."

"That's right. He did." Her head turned. "Charlotte?"

Miss Haber's mouth opened, and closed. She lifted a hand, and dropped it. "Please, Mrs. Odell," she said. "I don't think—You tell him. Please?"

"Well, you're here." Mrs. Odell went back to Wolfe. "There are strong people," she said, "and there are weak people, and Miss Haber is one of the weak ones. She's extremely competent, but weak. She found out for me how to get some LSD, and in fact she got it for me, about a month ago. Then she found out what I was going to do with it by eavesdropping on us—my husband and me. Then she phoned Amory Browning and told him what we were going to do. I didn't know that until three days after my husband died. So she was weak three times—getting the LSD for me without knowing what I wanted it for, and phoning Browning, and telling me. You said the most important question is who knew my husband was going to that room and open that drawer. All right, three people knew: Miss Haber and me, and

Amory Browning. And she told Browning four
days before it happened, so he had plenty of time
to get the bomb."

Wolfe was frowning at her with his chin down.
"A remarkable performance," he said. "Extraor-
dinary. You seem not to be aware that—"

She cut in. "I'm not through. About Browning
getting the bomb. Do you watch television?"

"Rarely."

"About three months ago, CAN had a one-
hour special they called 'Where the Little Bombs
Come From.' Did you see it?"

"No."

"Lots of people thought it told too much about
what bombs are made of and who makes them,
but it really didn't, because they changed all the
names and didn't give any addresses. That program was Browning's idea and his staff did all the
research, so getting one would have been easy for
him. If you mean it would have been remarkable
for him to get a bomb in four days and know how
to use it, it wouldn't."

Wolfe was still frowning. "I didn't mean that.
I meant *your* performance. That is of course one
detail to be considered, but before considering details I must know if I'm going to be concerned
with them. If I take the job, what do you expect
me to do?"

"I expect you to tell *me* what to do, and I suppose help me do it. I want Amory Browning in-
dicted and tried and convicted, but I do *not* want
what I have told you to be known. I am not going
to sit in a witness chair and tell what my husband
and I did and answer questions about it. How
many things have *you* done that you wouldn't
want everyone to know about?"

"Perhaps a thousand. Adulterating a rival's
whisky is not one of them, but tastes and methods
differ." Wolfe's head turned. "Miss Haber. Do you

corroborate what Mrs. Odell has told me of your share in this affair?"

The secretary swallowed. I had her in profile, but apparently her eyes were straight at him. She said "Yes," but it was barely audible, and she repeated it louder, "Yes, I do."

"You got some LSD at her request?"

"Yes, but I'm not going to tell how I got it."

"I don't need to know, at least not now. And you learned how she was going to use it by overhearing conversations she had with her husband?"

"Yes. I thought I had a right to know. LSD is illegal. It can't be sold legally and you can't even have it in your possession."

"And you decided to tell Mr. Browning about it? Why?"

"Because I was afraid it might kill him. The amount I got and gave Mrs. Odell—it was about four tablespoons—I didn't know what it would do. If the whisky bottle was only half full, or even less, and Mr. Odell put all that LSD in it—from the little I knew I thought it *would* kill him. I would be an accessory to a murder, and anyway I didn't want to help kill a man. It may be what Mrs. Odell said, that I'm one of the weak ones—anyhow, I didn't want to be a murderer."

"How did you communicate with Mr. Browning? Did you write to him?"

"I phoned him. I phoned him Friday evening, from a booth, at his place in the country. I didn't tell him my name. I didn't tell him *any* names. I just told him that Tuesday afternoon someone was going to put a dangerous drug in the whisky in his desk drawer and he had better not drink it. He wanted to ask questions, but I hung up. Of course I supposed he would suspect it would be Mr. Odell, but I certainly didn't suppose he would do what he did."

"Where is his country place?"

"In Connecticut. Westport."

"You say you phoned him Friday evening. Which Friday?"

"The Friday before it happened. Four days before."

"That was May sixteenth."

"Was it?" It took her only a moment, not a long one, to figure it. "That's right. May sixteenth."

"You phoned him at what hour?"

"Around nine o'clock. A little after nine. When I thought he would have finished dinner."

"How sure are you it was Mr. Browning?"

"Oh, *quite* sure. He answered the phone himself, and I know his voice. I have heard him on the phone at least a dozen times, when he has called Mr. Odell at home."

Wolfe regarded her. "And you didn't tell Mrs. Odell you had warned him."

"Of course not."

"But you did tell her, three days after Mr. Odell died. Why?"

"Because—well, I *had* to. I said I didn't want to be a murderer, but I *was* one. If I hadn't made that phone call, Mr. Odell would still be alive, and maybe Mr. Browning would too. The LSD might not have hurt him at all. To go right on being with Mrs. Odell every day—I *had* to tell her."

Wolfe turned to the prospective client. "That was two weeks ago. Why haven't you dismissed her?"

"That's a silly question," Mrs. Odell said. "She might tell anyone. She might tell the police. I'm not hiring you to analyze what Miss Haber has done—or what I have done. I want to know how we can make Browning pay for what *he* did without telling what *we* did."

Wolfe closed his eyes, and the forefinger of his right hand started making little circles on his desk blotter. But he wasn't tackling a tough one; his lips didn't move. So he had made his decision and was merely considering whether he should ask more questions before announcing it. In half a minute he quit making circles, lifted his hand to give his forehead a rub, and swiveled to look at me. If they hadn't been there he would have put it into words: "You got me into this. I concede the desirability of a fee, but you got me into *this*."

Having looked it, long enough to count ten, he swiveled back to her. "Very well. It's an impossible job, but I'll accept the retainer. My fee will be based on effort and risk, not on accomplishment. I'll need facts, many facts, but it's nearly dinner time, and anyway I want them at first hand. Archie, list these names: Mr. Browning. Mr. Abbott. Mr. Falk. Mr. Meer. Mrs. Browning. Miss Lugos. Miss Venner." Back to the client: "Will you have those people here tomorrow evening at nine o'clock?"

She stared at him. "I will not. How can I?"

"I don't know, but it shouldn't be too difficult. They were associates of your husband, who was murdered. They should be willing to help you learn who murdered him, and you are concerned at the lack of progress in the official investigation and have engaged my services. Shouldn't they sacrifice an evening at your request?"

"They might. I don't want to ask them. And I won't."

Wolfe picked up the check and held it out. "Take it. You have wasted your time and mine. You want a miracle, and miracles are not in my repertory. Give me the receipt."

"My god," she said, "you *are* highhanded. What can *they* tell you?"

"I don't know, and I need to know. If there is a fact that will help me do what you want done, I want it. If you think I may inadvertently disclose what you have told me, even a hint of it, if you think me capable of such ineptitude, you were a ninny to come to me at all."

She was chewing her lip. "Is this the only—do you *have* to do this?"

"If I take the job as you defined it, yes."

She looked at me, and saw only an open, intelligent, interested, sympathetic phiz.

"Damn it," she said. "Give me the list."

6

Since the state of the bank account had been responsible for the state of my nerves for at least six weeks, it might be supposed that ten o'clock Monday morning would find me at the door of the Continental Bank and Trust Company, waiting for it to open so I could deposit the check, but I wasn't. I knew darned well that Wolfe would not be firmly and finally committed until Mrs. Odell came through, and I couldn't blame him. Of the people on the list I had given her, there wasn't one that he could tell me to go and bring with any right or reason to expect me to fill the order, and if he expected to fill *her* order, he had to get some questions answered, and not just by her and Miss Haber. So it was possible that the twenty grand would have to be returned, and if so, it would be neater to return her check than to deposit it and then have to draw one of Wolfe's.

And at four o'clock Monday afternoon, it became about ten to one that she was going to get her check back. She had done fine with the invitations; she reported by phone that all of them had said yes. The hitch was that when she told me she would come a little early, around half past eight, I had to tell her, as instructed by Wolfe, that he had decided she shouldn't come at all. She wasn't invited and wouldn't be admitted. So she blew her top. I tried to explain why, but she wouldn't listen. She commanded me to get Wolfe to change his mind and ring her, and if she hadn't heard from me by four-thirty, she would tell them not to come. I went to the kitchen to tell Fritz I was going on an errand, ran, not walked, to the garage on Tenth Avenue where the Heron sedan that Wolfe owns and I drive is kept, made it to Sixty-third and Madison in nineteen minutes, probably a record for that time of day, and was inside the Odell mansion at 4:28. If I reported that conversation verbatim you would think I was tooting my horn, so I'll merely say that I sold her. I explained that when Browning told lies, as he surely would, if she was there she would almost certainly horn in, and if she expected Wolfe to get results she would have to let him do it his way. Also, of course, if she told them not to come, the deal was off and she would have to find someone who would do it her way, and obviously she didn't have any or she wouldn't have gone to Wolfe and given him a check for twenty grand. She didn't like it, but she lumped it.

Then, leaving, I got a break. I had had to double-park, on Sixty-third Street, and it was a pleasant surprise to see that no city employee had happened by to put a ticket on the windshield. The return trip took thirty-one minutes. When Wolfe came down at six o'clock and I reported, he didn't even say "Satisfactory." He merely scowled and rang for beer. His outlook was bleak. It was now settled that he was going to have to work, and with an obstreperous female for a client.

They all came. The first to arrive, Sylvia Venner, showed a little before nine, and the last, Kenneth Meer, at 9:08. Cass R. Abbott rated the red leather chair on two counts: he was the president of CAN, and, being close to seventy, he had seniority. So I put him there. For the others I had placed two rows of yellow chairs facing Wolfe's desk. I have a sort of rule that when there is company and one of them is, or is supposed to be, a murderer, the place for him or her is the front row nearest to me, so that was where I put Amory Browning. Next to him was his wife, and then Theodore Falk. In the back row Kenneth Meer was in the middle, with Helen Lugos on his right and Sylvia Venner on his left. The only one I had ever seen before was Kenneth Meer. When I let him in, he had looked me in the eye and asked, "More tricks?" and I said, "No, and we have made no use of that one. If anyone here knows about your bloody hands, he didn't learn it from us."

Since you're meeting them, you should see them. Cass R. Abbott, the president, looked like one. The mop of well-tended white hair, which he had a right to be proud of and probably was, was a good cap for the well-arranged, long, pale face. Amory Browning, who would soon be president if he wasn't otherwise engaged, didn't rate it on looks. If he was fifty-two, which would have been my guess, he had probably been pudgy for about five years, and he would be bald in another five. Theodore Falk, the Wall Street Falk, was about the same age, but he had kept himself lean and limber and had a deep tan. He probably played tennis. You have already seen Kenneth Meer's long, pointed nose and wide, square chin.

As for the females, I would have recognized Sylvia Venner from the dozen or so times I had seen her do "The Big Town," the program Browning had bounced her from. She was easy to look at, especially when she was using certain muscles to show her dimples, but TV girls, like all actresses, are always working at it and if you get really interested you have to make allowances. I don't want to be unfair to Mrs. Browning merely because our client had her husband tagged for murder, but the truth is she was scrawny. I could give details, but why rub it in? She was about her husband's age, and she was scrawny, and facts are facts. Helen Lugos, Browning's secretary, was the one you would have to see with your own eyes, because she was the kind with whom details like color of eyes and hair, and shape of face, and kind of mouth don't really tell it. She was probably three or four years under thirty, but that was only another unimportant detail. The point was that I had put her in the back row chair the other side of Kenneth Meer because that was where I could see her best and oftenest without turning my head much. I would have liked to put her in the red leather chair where I would have had her full face, but of course that was the president's place. Hers was the kind of face that is different from any two angles.

I had invited orders for liquids, but they had all been declined, and when Kenneth Meer was in and seated, I went to Wolfe's desk and gave the kitchen button three stabs, and in a moment he came, detoured between the red leather chair and the wall to his desk, sat, and sent his eyes around. As I pronounced the seven names, he gave each of them a nod—*his* nod, about an eighth of an inch.

"On behalf of Mrs. Odell," he said, "I thank you for coming. She intended to be here, but she conceded my point that her presence would make our discussion more difficult, both for you and for me. I know, of course, that you have all been questioned at length by officers of the law, and I shall not try to emulate them, either in pertinacity or in scope. I frankly admit that I strongly doubt if I'll get what Mrs. Odell wants. She hired me to learn who killed her husband, and the prospect is forlorn. Apparently no one knows whether his death was premeditated, or fortuitous—except the person who put the bomb in the drawer."

His eyes went right, then left. "What information I have has come from three sources: the newspapers, Mrs. Odell, and four or five journalists who have worked on the case and with whom

Mr. Goodwin is on friendly terms. There is no agreement among the opinions they have formed. One of them thinks that Mr. Odell went to that room and opened that drawer, and put the bomb in it, in order to—"

"Oh for god's sake." It was Theodore Falk. "That kind of crap?"

Wolfe nodded. "Certainly. In the effort to solve any complex problem, there are always many apparent absurdities; the job is to find the correct answer and demonstrate that it is *not* absurd. Another of the journalists thinks that Mr. Abbott put the bomb in the drawer because he didn't want Mr. Browning to succeed him as president of CAN. Still another thinks that Mrs. Browning did it, or arranged to have it done, because she didn't want her husband to continue to enjoy the favors of Miss Lugos. He hasn't decided whom it was intended for, Mr. Browning or Miss Lugos. And another thinks that Miss Lugos did it because she did want Mr. Browning to continue to enjoy her favors but he—"

"Tommyrot!" Cass R. Abbott, in the red leather chair, blurted it. "I came because Mrs. Odell asked me to, but not to hear a list of idiotic absurdities. She said you wanted to get some facts from us. What facts?"

Wolfe turned a palm up. "How do I know? All of you have been questioned at length by the police; you have given them thousands of facts, and in assembling, comparing and evaluating a collection of facts they are well practiced and extremely competent. It's possible that from the record of all the questions they have asked, and your answers to them, I might form a surmise or reach a conclusion that they have failed to see, but I doubt it. I confess to you, though I didn't to Mrs. Odell, that I have little hope of getting useful facts from you. What I needed, to begin at all, was to see you and hear you. It seems likely that one of you put the bomb in the drawer. There are other possibilities, but probabilities have precedence. A question, Mr. Abbott: Do you think it likely that the person who put the bomb in the drawer is now in this room?"

"That's absurd," Abbott snapped. "I wouldn't answer that and you know it."

"But you *have* answered it. You didn't give me a positive no, and you're a positive man." Wolfe's eyes went right. "Mr. Falk. Do you think it likely?"

"Yes, I do," Falk said, "and I could name names, three of them, but I won't. I have no evidence, but I have an opinion, and that's what you asked for."

"I don't expect names. Mrs. Browning. The same question."

"Don't answer, Phyllis," Browning said. A command.

"Of course not. I wasn't going to." Her voice didn't match her scrawniness; it was a full, rich contralto, with color.

Wolfe asked, "Then you, Mr. Browning? Are you going to answer?"

"Yes. I'll tell you exactly what I have told the police and the District Attorney. I not only have no evidence, I have no basis whatever for an opinion. Not even an opinion as to whether the bomb was intended for me or for Odell. It was my room and my desk, but the fact remains that it was Odell who got it. I'll also tell you that I am not surprised that Mrs. Odell has engaged you, and I don't blame her. After nearly three weeks the official investigation is apparently completely stymied."

Wolfe nodded. "I *may* have better luck. Miss Lugos? The same question."

"The same as Mr. Browning," she said. I acknowledge that her voice wasn't as good as Mrs. Browning's; it was thinner and pitched higher. "I have no idea. None at all." Also she wasn't a good

liar. When you have asked about ten thousand
people about a million questions you may not be
able to spot a lie as well as you think you can, but
you're right a lot oftener than you're wrong.

"Mr. Meer?"

Naturally I was wondering about Kenneth
Meer. Like everybody who reads about murders in
newspapers, I knew that he had been the fourth
or fifth person to enter Browning's room after the
explosion, so he had seen blood all right, but that
alone wouldn't account for the blood-on-his-hands
crisis that had sent him to the clinic, unless he had
bad kinks in his nervous system, bad enough to
keep him from working up to such an important
job at CAN and hanging onto it. There was the
obvious possibility that he had planted the bomb,
but surely not for Browning, and if for Odell, how
did he know Odell was going to the room and open
the drawer? Of course Mrs. Odell had made the
answer to that one easy: Browning had told him.
Now, how would he answer Wolfe's question?

He answered it with a declaration which he
had had plenty of time to decide on: "I think it
extremely likely that the person who put the bomb
in the drawer is now in this room, but that's all I
can say. I can't give any reason or any name."

"You can't, or you won't?"

"Does it matter? Just make it I don't."

"But I ask you if—no. That will come later, if
at all. Miss Venner?"

She wasn't showing the dimples. Instead, she
had been squinting at Wolfe, and still was. "I don't
get it," she said. "I don't think you are dumb, but
this is dumb, and I wonder why you're doing it.
Even if I thought I could name the person who
put the bomb in the drawer, would I tell you with
them here? Mr. Abbott is the head of the company
that employs me, and Mr. Browning is going to
be. I can't, but even if I could . . . I don't get it."

"You haven't listened," Wolfe told her. "I said

that I had little hope of getting any useful facts from you, and I could have added that even if I do, you probably won't know it. For instance, the question I ask you now. About three months ago CAN had a special program called 'Where the Little Bombs Come From.' Did you see it?"

"Yes. Of course."

"Then you know that the preparation for that program required extensive research. There had to be numerous contacts between members of the CAN staff and people who knew about bombs and had had experience with them. Call them the *sources*. Now I ask you regarding three weeks ago —Friday, May sixteenth, to Sunday, May eighteenth—where and how did you spend that weekend? It may help to remember that the Tuesday following, two days later, Mr. Odell died."

"But why do you—" She wasn't squinting; her eyes were wide in a stare. "Oh. You think I went to one of the 'sources' and got a bomb. Well, I didn't."

"I don't 'think' anything. I'm trying to get a start for a thought. I asked where and how you spent that weekend. Have you a reason for not telling me?"

"No. I have no reason for telling you either, but I might as well. I've told the police four or five times. I took a train to Katonah late Friday afternoon and was a house guest of friends— Arthur and Louise Dickinson. They know nothing about bombs. I came back by train Sunday evening."

I had got my notebook and a pen and was using them. Wolfe asked, "Mr. Meer? Have you any objection to telling me how you spent that weekend?"

"Certainly not. I drove to Vermont Friday evening and I hiked about forty miles in the mountains Saturday and Sunday, and drove back Sunday night."

"Alone, or with companions?"

"I was alone. I don't like companions on a hike. Something always happens to them. I helped some with the research for that program, and none of the 'sources' was in Vermont."

"I am hoping that Mr. Browning will tell me about the sources. Later. Miss Lugos?"

Her face was really worth watching. As he pronounced her name, she turned her head for a glance at Browning, her boss. It was less than a quarter-turn, but from my angle it wasn't the same face as when she was looking at Wolfe. Her look at Browning didn't seem to be asking or wanting anything; evidently it was just from habit. She turned back to Wolfe and said, "I stayed in town all that weekend. Friday evening I went to a movie with a friend. Saturday afternoon I did some shopping, and Saturday evening I went to a show with three friends. Sunday I got up late and did things in my apartment. In a file at the office we have a record of all the research for that program, all the people who were contacted, and I didn't see any of them that weekend."

Wolfe's lips were tight. In his house, "contact" is not a verb and never will be, and he means it. He was glad to quit her. "Mr. Falk?"

Falk had been holding himself in, shifting in his chair and crossing and uncrossing his legs. Obviously he thought it was *all* crap. "You said," he said, "that you wouldn't try to emulate the police, but that's what you're doing. But Peter Odell was my best and closest friend, and there may be a chance that you're half as good as you're supposed to be. As for that weekend, I spent it at home— my place on Long Island. We had four house guests—no, five—and none of them was a bomb expert. Do you want their names and addresses?"

"I may, later." As Wolfe's eyes went to Mrs. Browning, her husband spoke: "My wife and I were together that weekend. We spent it on a yacht on the Sound, guests of the man who owns it, James Farquhar, the banker. There were two other guests."

"The whole weekend, Mr. Browning?"

"Yes. From late Friday afternoon to late Sunday afternoon."

I put my eyes on my notebook and kept them there. With all the practice I have had with my face, I should of course always have it under control, but I had got two jolts, not just one. First, was that why Wolfe had started the whole rigmarole about that weekend, to check on Browning, and second, had Browning heard it coming and got set for it, or had he just given a straight answer to a straight question? I don't know how well Wolfe handled *his* face, since my eyes were on my notebook, but otherwise he did fine. There were two or three other questions he must have wanted to ask Browning, but he didn't. He merely remarked that he doubted if Mr. Farquhar or the other guests were in the bomb business and then said, "And you, Mr. Abbott?" and my eyes left the notebook.

"I resent this," Abbott said. "I knew Pete Odell for twenty years and we worked together for ten of them, and I have a warm and deep sympathy for his wife, his widow, but this is ridiculous. I assumed you would have some new angle, some new approach, but all you're doing, you're starting the same old grind. Each of us has spent long hours with the police, answering questions and signing statements, and while we want to oblige Mrs. Odell, naturally we do, I certainly don't think she should expect us to repeat the whole performance with you. Why doesn't she ask the police to let you see their files? In one of them you'll find out how I spent that weekend. I spent it at home, near Tarrytown. There were guests. I played golf all day and bridge at night. But I repeat, this is ridiculous."

A corner of Wolfe's mouth was up. "Then it would be fruitless to continue," he said—not complaining, just stating a fact. He put his hands on the edge of his desk for purchase, pushed his chair back, and rose. "I'll have to contrive a new approach. On behalf of Mrs. Odell, I thank you again for coming. Good evening." He moved, detoured again between the wall and the red leather chair, and, out in the hall, turned left.

"I'll be damned," Theodore Falk said.

I think they all said things, but if any of it was important, that will be a gap in this report. I wasn't listening, as I went through the appropriate motions for godspeeding a flock of guests. I had heard enough, more than enough, for one evening. I didn't even notice who went with whom as they descended the seven steps of the stoop to the sidewalk. Closing the door and sliding the chainbolt in its slot, I went to the kitchen. Fritz, who had kept handy to fill orders for refreshments if called for, was perched on the stool by the big center table with a magazine, but his eyes weren't on it. They were on Wolfe, who was standing, scowling at a glass of beer in his hand, waiting for the bead to settle to the right level.

"It's going on eleven o'clock," I said. "I would love to start on it right now, but I suppose I can't."

"Of course not," he growled. He drank beer. "Do we need to discuss it?"

"I don't think so." I went and got a bottle of scotch from the cupboard. There are times when milk will not do. "I have a suggestion. Do you want it?"

He said yes, and I gave it to him.

7

At five minutes past eleven Tuesday morning, I was seated in a comfortable chair at the end of a big, expensive desk in a big, expensive room on the thirtieth floor of a big, expensive building on Broad Street, near Wall, facing a man whose tan was much deeper than Theodore Falk's—so deep that his hide might have been bronze.

Getting to him had been simple, but first I had had to confirm that he existed and owned a yacht. At one minute past nine I had dialed the number of the magazine *Fore and Aft;* no answer. Modern office hours. Half an hour later I got them, and was told by a man, after I held the wire while he looked it up, that a man named James J. Farquhar had a fifty-eight-foot Derecktor cruiser named *Prospero.* So it was a yacht, not just a rowboat with a mast or an outboard motor. Next I dialed the number of the Federal Holding Corporation, and via two women and a man, which was par, got through to Avery Ballou. He sounded as if he still remembered what Wolfe and I had done for him three years ago, and still appreciated it. I told him we needed a little favor and asked if he knew a banker named James Farquhar.

"Sure," he said. "He's next to the top at Trinity Fiduciary. What has he done?"

"As far as I know, nothing. It isn't another

paternity problem. I want to ask him a couple of questions about something that he's not involved in—and he won't be. He's the best bet for a piece of information we need, that's all. But the sooner we get it, the better, and Mr. Wolfe thought you might be willing to ring him and tell him that if I phone him for an appointment, it would be a good idea for him to tell me to come right away and get rid of me."

He said he would, and ten minutes later his secretary phoned and said Farquhar was expecting a call from me. She even gave me the phone number, and I dialed it and got *his* secretary.

So at 11:05 there I was, at his desk. I was apologizing. "Mr. Wolfe didn't want to bother you," I said, "about a matter that you will consider trivial, but he sort of had to. It's about something that happened more than three weeks ago—Friday, May sixteenth. A lawyer has a client who is being sued for damages, fifty thousand dollars, and he has asked Mr. Wolfe to check on a couple of things. The client's name is O'Neill, Roger O'Neill, and a man named Walsh claims that around half past eight that evening he was in his small boat, fishing in the Sound, near Madison, about a mile off shore, and O'Neill's big cruiser came along fast, doing at least twenty, he says, and hit his boat right in the middle—cut it right in two. The sun had set but it wasn't dark yet, and Walsh says he had a light up. He wasn't hurt much, but his twelve-year-old son was; he's still in the hospital."

Farquhar was frowning. "But where do I come in? I have a busy morning."

"I'm keeping it as brief as possible. Walsh says there were witnesses. He says a bigger boat, around seventy feet, was cruising by, about two hundred yards farther out, and there were people on deck who must have seen it happen. He tried to see its name, but he was in the water and the light was dim. He thinks it was *Properoo*." I spelled it. "We can't find a boat with that name listed anywhere, but your yacht, *Prospero,* comes close to it. Friday, May sixteenth. Three weeks ago last Friday. Were you out on the Sound that day?"

"I'm out *every* Friday. That Friday . . . three weeks . . ." He shut his eyes and tilted his head back. "That was . . . No. . . . Oh, sure." His eyes opened and his head leveled. "I was across the Sound. Nowhere near Madison. Before nine o'clock we anchored in a cove near Stony Brook, on the other shore."

"Then it wasn't you." I stood up. "Have you ever seen a boat named *Properoo?*"

"No."

"If you don't mind—Mr. Wolfe always expects me to get everything. Who was on board with you?"

"My wife, and four guests. Mr. and Mrs. Percy Young, and Mr. and Mrs. Amory Browning. And the crew, two. Really, damn it—"

"Okay. I'm sorry I bothered you for nothing, and Mr. Wolfe will be too. Many thanks."

I went.

In the elevator, going down, a woman moved away from me, clear away. I wasn't bothering to manage my face, and probably its expression indicated that I was all set to choke or shoot somebody. I was. Down in the lobby I went to a phone booth and dialed the number I knew best, and when Fritz answered I said, "Me. I want him."

It took a couple of minutes. It always does; he hates the phone.

"Yes, Archie?"

"I'm in a booth in a building on Broad Street. I have just had a talk with James J. Farquhar. At nine o'clock Friday evening, May sixteenth, he anchored his yacht in a cove on the Long Island shore. The four guests aboard were Mr. and Mrs. Percy Young and Mr. and Mrs. Amory Browning.

I'm calling because it's nearly eleven-thirty, and if I proceed as instructed I couldn't have her there in less than an hour, which would be too close to lunch. I suggest that I phone her instead of going to get her, and—"

"No. Come home. I'll telephone her. The number?"

"On my yellow pad in the middle drawer. But wouldn't it—"

"No." He hung up.

So he too was set for murder. He was going to dial it himself. He was going to risk keeping lunch waiting. As I headed for the subway, which would be quicker than scouting for a taxi in that territory, I was trying to remember if any other client, male or female, had ever equaled this, and couldn't name one.

But when I entered the old brownstone, and the office, a few minutes before noon, I saw he wasn't going to choke her or shoot her. He was going to slice her up. At his desk, with his oilstone and a can of oil on a sheet of paper, he was sharpening his penknife. Though he doesn't use it much, he sharpens it about once a week, but almost never at that time of day. Evidently his subconscious had taken over. I went to my desk and sat, opened a drawer and took out the Marley .38, and asked, "Do I shoot her before you carve her, or after?"

He gave me a look. "How likely is it that Mr. Browning telephoned him last night, or saw him, and arranged it?"

"No. A hundred to one. I took my time with a phony buildup and watched his face. Also at least seven other people would have to be arranged: his wife, the four guests, and the crew. Not a chance. You got Miss Haber?"

"Yes." He looked at the clock. "Thirty-five minutes ago. I made it—"

The doorbell rang. I put the Marley in the

57

drawer and closed it, and went. But in the hall,
I saw more than I expected. I stepped back in and
asked Wolfe, "Did you invite Mrs. Odell too?"

"No."

"Then she invited herself. She came along.
So?"

He shut his eyes, opened them, shut them,
opened them. "Very well. You may have to drag
her to the front room."

That would have been a pleasure—preferably
by the hair with her kicking and screaming. She
performed as expected. When I opened the front
door, she brushed past me rudely and streaked
down the hall, with Miss Haber at her tail, trot-
ting to keep up. Thinking she might actually
scratch or bite, I was right behind as she entered
the office and opened up, heading for Wolfe's desk.
I'm not sure whether the five words she got out
were "If you think you can" or "If you think
you're going," before Wolfe banged a fist on the
desk and bellowed at her:

"Shut up!"

I don't know how he does it. His bellow is
a loud explosion, a boom, as a bellow should be,
but also it has an edge, it cuts, which doesn't seem
possible. She stopped and stood with her mouth
open. I was between her and him.

"I told Miss Haber to come," Wolfe said in his
iciest tone. "Not you. If you sit and listen, you
may stay. If you don't, Mr. Goodwin will remove
you—from the room and the house. He would enjoy it. I have something to say to Miss Haber, and
I will not tolerate interruption. Well?"

Her mouth was even wider than normal because her teeth were clamped on her lower lip.
She moved, not fast, toward the red leather chair,
but Wolfe snapped, "No. I want Miss Haber in
that chair. Archie?"

I went and brought a yellow chair and put it
closer to my desk than his. She gave me a look that

I did not deserve, and came and sat. I doubted if Charlotte Haber would make it to the red leather chair without help, so I went and touched her arm, and steered her to it.

Wolfe's eyes at her were only slits. "I told you on the telephone," he said, "that if you were not here by twelve o'clock, I would telephone a policeman, Inspector Cramer of Homicide South, and tell him what you told me Sunday evening about your telephone call to Mr. Browning on May sixteenth. I'll probably find it necessary to tell him anyway, but I thought it proper to give you a chance to explain. Why did you tell me that lie?"

She was making a fair try at meeting his eyes. She spoke: "It wasn't—" Her tongue got in the way and she stopped and started over: "It wasn't a lie. It was exactly like I told you. If Mr. Browning won't admit it, if he denies—"

"Pfui. I haven't discussed it with Mr. Browning. The conclusive evidence that you couldn't have made that call did not come from him. Even candor may not serve you now, but certainly nothing else will. Unless you tell me what and who induced you to tell me that lie, you're in for it. You'll leave here not with your employer, but with a policeman, probably for detention as a material witness. I will not—"

"You can't!" Mrs. Odell was on the edge of her chair. "You know you can't! You guaranteed in writing!"

"Remove her, Archie," Wolfe said. "If necessary, drag her."

I rose. She tilted her head to focus up at me and said, "You don't dare. Don't dare to touch me."

I said, "I dare easy. I admit I'd rather not, but I have bounced bigger and stronger women than you and have no scars. Look. You tried to steal home and got nailed, and no wonder. You didn't even have sense enough to check where

59

Browning was that Friday night. As for that guarantee in that receipt you got, it says, quote, 'Unless circumstances arise that put me or him under legal compulsion to reveal it.' End quote. Okay, the circumstances are here. The cops have spent a thousand hours trying to find out why your husband went to the room and opened the drawer, and who knew he was going to. Now *I* know. So I'm withholding essential evidence in a murder case, and there's a statute that puts me under legal compulsion to reveal it. Also, I'm not just a law-abiding citizen, I'm a licensed private detective, and I don't want to lose my license and have to start a new career, like panhandling or demonstrating. So even if Mr. Wolfe got big-hearted and decided just to bow out, there would still be me. I feel responsible. I *am* responsible. I started this by writing you that letter. Mr. Wolfe told Miss Haber that unless she comes clean he will open the bag. I may or may not stay with him on the *unless*. I am good and sore, and for a dirty crinkled dollar bill with a corner gone I would go now to the drug store on the corner and ring a police sergeant I know. I also know a man on the *Gazette* who would love to have a hot item for the front page, and I could back it up with an affidavit. And would."

I turned to Wolfe. "If I may offer a suggestion. If you still want her bounced, okay, but from her face I think she has got it down."

I turned back to her. "If you get the idea that you can say it was *all* a lie, that you wanted to fasten it on Browning and made it *all* up, nothing doing. They found the LSD in your husband's pocket and they've got it. You're stuck, absolutely, and if you try to wriggle you'll just make it worse."

She had kept her eyes at me. Now they went to her right, clear around past Wolfe to Miss Haber, and they certainly saw nothing helpful.

Below the crease in the narrow forehead, the secretary's eyes weren't aimed anywhere. They could have been seeing her hands clasped on her lap, but probably they weren't seeing anything.

Mrs. Odell aimed hers at Wolfe. "You said you haven't discussed it with Browning. The—the LSD. Who have you discussed it with?"

"Mr. Goodwin. No one else."

"Then how did you—How can you—"

"Mr. Goodwin talked this morning with a man who owns a yacht. At nine o'clock in the evening of Friday, May sixteenth, when he anchored in a cove on the Long Island shore, two of the guests aboard were Mr. and Mrs. Amory Browning. In all my experience with chicanery, madam, I have never encountered a more inept performance. A factor in our animus is probably the insult to our intelligence; you should have known that we would inquire as to Mr. Browning's whereabouts that evening, and therefore *you* should have. By the glance you just gave Miss Haber I suspect that you are contemplating another inanity: saying it was some other evening. Pfui. Don't try it. Look at Miss Haber."

She didn't have to; she already had. And she proceeded to demonstrate that she was by no means a complete fool. She cocked her head at me for a long, steady look, and then cocked it at Wolfe. "I don't believe," she said, "that you have really decided to tell the police about it. If you had, you wouldn't have phoned Miss Haber and—"

"I haven't said I have decided. I said, to Miss Haber, 'Unless you tell me what and who induced you to tell that lie.'"

"*I'll* tell you. *I* induced her."

"When?"

"Three days ago. Saturday evening. And Sunday morning, before I called Goodwin. *What* induced her was money. She needs money. She has a younger brother who has got himself into—but

61

that doesn't matter, what she needs it for. And anyway, I think Browning put that bomb there. I'm *sure* he did. I don't know how he knew Peter was going to open that drawer, but I'm sure he did. Maybe Peter told somebody. You didn't know Peter, you don't know what a wonderful man he was. He married me for my money, but he was a wonderful husband. And Browning killed him, and with all the money I have, now there's only one thing I want to do with it. I don't think the police will ever get him, and you know something they don't know. Can you handle Goodwin?"

"No." He was scowling at her. "No one can 'handle' Mr. Goodwin. But he handles himself reasonably well, and he wouldn't divulge information he got as my agent without my consent. My problem is handling me. Your fatuous attempt to hoodwink me relieves me of my commitment, but I too am a licensed private detective. If Mr. Cramer learns that those seven people were here last evening, as he probably will, and if he comes to see me, as he almost certainly will, I'll be in a pickle. I have many times refused to disclose information on the ground that it was not material, but the fact that your husband went to that room and opened that drawer in order to put LSD in the whisky is manifestly material. Confound it, they even have the LSD—that is, you *say* they have it."

"They do. They showed it to me." She opened her bag and took out the checkfold. "I've made one idiotic mistake with you and I don't intend to make another one. I'm going to give you a check for one hundred thousand dollars, but I have sense enough to know that I have to be careful how I do it. If you think that I think I can pay you and Goodwin for not telling the police about the LSD, I don't. I know I can't. But I do think they will never get Browning, and I think you might. I think the only chance of getting him is if you do it. I don't care what it costs. The hundred thousand dollars is just to start. You may have to give somebody twice that much for something." She slid the pen out and started to write on the check stub.

"No," Wolfe said. "You can't pay me at all on the terms you imply. I certainly would not engage to demonstrate that Mr. Browning killed your husband. I might engage to try to learn *who* killed your husband and to get evidence that would convict him. As for withholding information from the police, that must be left to my discretion. Mr. Goodwin and I are disinclined to share with others information that gives us an advantage."

"It *was* Browning. Why do you think it wasn't?"

"I don't. He is as likely a candidate as anyone —much the most likely, if he knew of your husband's intention to drug the whisky." He swiveled to face the red leather chair. "Miss Haber. You didn't tell Mr. Browning about it, but whom did you tell?"

"Nobody." It came out louder than she intended, and she repeated it, lower. "Nobody."

"This is extremely important. I *must* know. This time you are expected to tell me the truth."

"I *am* telling you the truth. I *couldn't* have told anyone because I didn't know myself. I didn't know what the LSD was for until last Saturday evening, three days ago, when Mrs. Odell told me ... When she asked me . . ."

Wolfe turned to Mrs. Odell with his brow up.

"*I* believe her," she said, and he turned back to the secretary.

"Do you go to church, Miss Haber?"

"Yes, I do. Lutheran. Not every Sunday, but often."

He turned to me. "Bring a Bible."

On the third shelf from the bottom, at the left of the globe, there were nine of them, four in dif-

ferent editions in English and five in foreign
languages. I picked the one that looked the part
best, in black leather, and crossed to the red
leather chair.

"Put your right hand on it," Wolfe told her,
"and repeat after me: With my hand on the Holy
Bible I swear."

I held it at her level and she put her hand on
it, palm down, flat, the fingers spread a little.
"With my hand on the Holy Bible I swear."

"That I did not know what Mr. Odell intended
to do."

She repeated it.

"With the LSD I had procured from Mrs.
Odell."

She repeated it.

"Until Saturday, June seventh."

She repeated it.

Wolfe turned to the client. "You can suspect
Mr. Browning only if you assume that he knew
what your husband was going to do. Miss Haber
didn't. I don't suppose you or your husband told
him. Whom did you tell?"

"I didn't tell anybody. Absolutely nobody. So
Peter must have. I wouldn't have thought—but he
must have. Of course there were people who
wanted Peter to be the new president, not Browning, and he must have told one of them. For instance, Ted Falk, but Ted wouldn't have told
Browning. I can give you names. Sylvia Venner.
Then there's a man in public relations—"

"If you please." He had turned his head to
look at the wall clock. "It's my lunch time. You
can make a list of the names, with relevant comments. But there must be no misunderstanding
about what you expect me to do. My commitment
is to try to learn who killed your husband and get
evidence that will convict him. Just that. Is that
clearly understood?"

"Yes. But I want to be sure . . . No. I suppose I can't be." She opened the checkfold. "But if it wasn't Browning . . . Oh, damn it. *God damn it.*" She wrote the check.

8

At twenty minutes to seven, Theodore Falk, in the red leather chair with his legs crossed, told Wolfe, "It would depend on what it was he was going to do."

In the four and a half hours since lunch, much had been done but nothing visible had been accomplished. We had discussed the Cramer problem. If and when he came, I could open the door only the two inches the chain on the bolt allowed and tell him Wolfe wasn't available and there was no telling when he would be, and I was under instructions to tell nobody anything whatever. He probably couldn't get a warrant, since all he could tell a judge was that some of the people involved in a murder case had spent part of an evening in the house, but if he did, and used it, we would stand mute—or sit mute. Or I could open the door wide and let him in, and Wolfe would play it by ear, and we voted for that. There was always a chance that he would supply one or more useful facts.

We had also decided to spend thirty-one dollars an hour, for as long as necessary, of the client's money, on Saul Panzer, Fred Durkin, and Orrie Cather—eight each for Fred and Orrie, and fifteen for Saul. If no one had known that Odell intended to go to Browning's room, the bomb couldn't have been intended for him, and it was going to take more doing than having people come to the old brownstone for some conversation. I had phoned Saul and Orrie and asked them to come Wednesday at ten o'clock, and left a message for Fred. And I had phoned Theodore Falk, Odell's best and closest friend, and told him that Wolfe wanted to have a talk with him, without an audience, and he said he would come around six o'clock.

By a couple of phone calls—one to a vice-president of our bank and one to Lon Cohen—I had learned that Falk was way up. He was a senior member of one of the oldest and solidest investment firms and sat on eight boards of directors. He had a wife and three grown-up children, and he and they were also solid socially. Evidently a man the race could be proud of, and from personal observation the only thing I had against him was his buttoned-down shirt collar. A man who hates loose flaps so much that he buttons down his collar should also button down his ears.

He came at 6:34.

Wolfe told him that he needed all the information he could get about Odell. Specifically, he needed the answer to a question: If Odell decided to do something secretly, some shabby deed that would help him and hurt someone else, how likely was it that he would have told anyone? And Falk said, "It would depend on what it was he was going to do. You say 'shabby'?"

Wolfe nodded. "Opprobrious. Mean. Furtive. Knavish. Tricky."

Falk uncrossed his legs, slid his rump clear back in the red leather chair, which is deep, recrossed his legs, and tilted his head back. His eyes went left and then right, in no hurry, apparently comparing the pictures on the wall—one of Socrates, one of Shakespeare, and an unwashed coal miner in oil by Sepeshy. (According to Wolfe, man's three resources: intellect, imagination, and muscle.)

In half a minute Falk's head leveled and his eyes settled on Wolfe. "I don't know about you," he said. "I don't know you well enough. A cousin of mine who is an assistant district attorney says you are sharp and straight. Does he know?"

"Probably not," Wolfe said. "Hearsay."

"You solicited Mrs. Odell."

I cut in. "No," I said. "I did."

Wolfe grunted. "Not material." To Falk: "Mr. Goodwin is my agent, and what he does is on my tally. He knew my bank balance was low. Does your firm solicit?"

Falk laughed, showing his teeth, probably knowing how white they looked with his deep tan. "Of course," he said, "you're not a member of the bar." He lifted a hand to rub his lip with a finger tip. That helped him decide to say something, and he said it. "You know that the police have a vial of LSD that was in Odell's pocket."

"Do I?"

"Certainly. Mrs. Odell has told me that she told you. Has she told you what he was going to do with it?"

"I'm sharp, Mr. Falk."

"So you are. Of course you'll tell her what I say, but she already knows that I think she knew what Pete was going to do with the LSD, though she won't admit it, and no wonder, not even to me."

"And you knew."

"I knew what?"

"What he was going to do with the LSD."

"No, I didn't. I don't know even now, but I can make a damn good guess, and so can the police. So can you, if Mrs. Odell hasn't told you. Going to Browning's room and opening that drawer, with LSD in his pocket? Better than a guess. You would call it shabby and opprobrious for him to dope Browning's whisky? And knavish?"

"Not to judge, merely to describe. Do you disagree?"

"I guess not. Not really. Anyway another good guess is that it was her idea, not his. You can tell her I said that, she already knows it. Of course your question is, did I know about it, did he tell me? He didn't. He wouldn't. If he told anybody it would have been me, but a thing like that he wouldn't tell even me. The reason I'm telling you this, I'm beginning to doubt if the police are going to crack it, and you might. One reason you might, Mrs. Odell will probably tell you things she won't tell them. Another reason is that with people like these, like us, the police have to consider things that you can ignore."

"And you want it cracked."

"Hell yes. Pete Odell was my favorite man."

"If no one knew he was going to open that drawer, he died by inadvertence."

"But whoever planted that bomb killed him." Falk turned a palm up. "Look, why am I here? This will make me an hour late for something. I wanted to know if you were going to waste time on the idea that the bomb was *intended* for Odell. The police still think it could have been and there's not a chance. Damn it, I *knew* him. It just isn't thinkable that he would have told anyone he was going to try to bust Browning by doping his whisky."

"If he had told you, would you have tried to dissuade him?"

Falk shook his head. "I can't even discuss it as a hypothesis. If Pete Odell had told me that, I would just have stared at him. It wouldn't have been him. Not his doing it, his telling me."

"So the bomb was for Browning?"

"Yes. Apparently."

"Not certainly?"

"No. You told us yesterday that the journalists have different ideas, and we have too—I mean the people who are involved. They are all just guessing really—except one of course, the one who did it. My guess is no better than anybody else's."

"And no worse. Your guess?"

Falk's eyes came to me and returned to Wolfe. "This isn't being recorded?"

"Only in our skulls."

"Well—do you know the name Copes? Dennis Copes?"

"No."

"You know Kenneth Meer. He was here last evening. He's Browning's man Friday, and Copes would like to be. Of course in a setup like CAN, most of them want someone else's job, but the Copes-Meer thing is special. My guess is that Meer had a routine of checking that drawer every afternoon and Copes knew it. Copes did a lot of work on that program about bombs and getting one would have been no problem. That's my best guess partly because I can't quite see anyone going for Browning with a bomb. A dozen people *could* have, but I can't see any of them actually doing it. You said one of the reporters thinks it was Browning's wife, but that's absurd."

"Did Kenneth Meer check the drawer every day?"

"I don't know. I understand he says he didn't."

I could fill three or four pages with the things Theodore Falk didn't know, but they didn't help us, so they wouldn't help you. When I returned to the office after going to the hall to let him out, we didn't discuss him, for two reasons: the look we exchanged showed that we didn't need to, and Fritz came to announce dinner. The look was a question, the same question both ways: How straight was Falk? Did we cross him off or not? The look left it open.

The fact was, Wolfe hadn't really bit into it. It was still just batting practice. He had taken the job and was committed, but there was still the slim chance that something might happen—the cops might get it or the client might quit—so he wouldn't have to sweat and slave. Also in my book there was the idea that I had once mentioned to him, the idea that it took a broil with Inspector Cramer to wind him up. Of course when I had offered it, he had fired me, or I had quit, I forget which. But I hadn't dropped the idea, so when the doorbell rang at 11:10 Wednesday morning and I went to the hall and saw who it was on the stoop through the one-way glass, and stepped back in the office and said "Mr. Fuzz," I didn't mind a bit.

Wolfe made a face, opened his mouth and then clamped his jaw, and in five seconds unclamped it to growl, "Bring him."

9

t hat was a first—the first time Inspector Cramer had ever arrived and been escorted to the office in the middle of a session with the hired hands. And Saul Panzer did something he seldom does—he stunted. He was in the red leather chair, and when I ushered Cramer in I expected to find Saul on his feet, moving up another yellow chair to join Fred and Orrie, but no. He was staying put. Cramer, surprised, stood in the middle of the rug and said, loud, "Oh?" Wolfe, surprised at Saul, put his brows up. I, pretending I wasn't surprised, went to get a yellow chair. And damned if Cramer didn't cross in front of Fred and Orrie to *my* chair, swing it around, and park his big fanny on it. As he sat, Saul, his lips a little tight to keep from grinning, got up and came to take the yellow chair I had brought. That left the red leather chair empty and I went and occupied it, sliding back and crossing my legs to show that I was right at home.

Wolfe didn't merely turn his head left to face me; he swiveled. "Was this performance arranged?" he demanded.

"Not by me," I told him. "This chair was empty, that's all."

"I guess I was just too surprised to move,"

Saul said. "I didn't know the Inspector was coming."

"Balls," Cramer said. "No one knew I was coming." He focused on Wolfe. "I hope I'm not interrupting anything important."

"I hope you are," Wolfe said, not thorny. "We are discussing the prospect of making an important contribution to the investigation of a murder."

Cramer nodded. "Yeah. I thought you would be."

Actually the discussion had barely begun. Saul Panzer, who looks like a guy who was trying to sell encyclopedias but gave up and quit, and is actually the best operative alive; and big-footed, heavy-set Fred Durkin, who looks as if he wouldn't know what an encyclopedia is but actually bought a Britannica for his kids; and good-looking, six-foot Orrie Cather, who would trade an encyclopedia for a full-length mirror if he didn't already have one, but can handle a tough assignment when he needs to, had come in at ten o'clock, and I had briefed them good. On some jobs they are called in on, some details have to be reserved, but not that one. I had given them the whole picture, and Wolfe, coming down from the plant rooms at eleven o'clock, had just got started.

When Wolfe faced Cramer in my chair with me in the red leather chair, I had his profile from his left instead of his right, and I had to adjust to it. I don't know why it made so much difference, but it did. His chin looked more pointed and his hair thicker. He asked Cramer politely, "You have questions?"

"Nothing specific." Cramer was leaning back, comfortable, also polite. "Don't mind me. Go right ahead." Saul's stunt had cued him.

Wolfe's eyes passed Orrie and Saul to Fred. "I was asking," he said, "if Archie covered the ground to your satisfaction. Do you need more?"

"I hope not." Fred riffled the pages of his notebook. "No room for more."

"What do you suggest?"

That routine was nearly always just talk, but now and then it led to something. "Well," Fred said, "you can't just walk up to the counter at Macy's and say one Number Four gelignite bomb and charge my account and don't bother to wrap it." He looked straight at Cramer. "What the hell."

Wolfe nodded. "No doubt the police have made every effort. Twenty-two days. Three weeks yesterday. You suggest . . . ?"

"I need time to sort it out."

"Yes. Orrie?"

"I need more," Orrie said. "For instance, I need to know if Odell had gloves on. One theory is that he was putting the bomb in the drawer to get Browning, and if so, he would have used gloves if he wasn't a moron. I suggest that you ask Inspector Cramer if he was wearing gloves, and if not, that will narrow it. Also you can ask him about fingerprints."

"Anything else?"

"Maybe. After I know that."

"Saul?"

"I may as well say it," Saul said. "Maybe it wasn't just surprise. I had a suggestion ready and the Inspector coming flipped me. I was going to say that if you asked for a look at the files, both Homicide and the DA, they might want to cooperate. After three weeks they must have quite a stack of stuff that—"

"Shove it," Cramer growled. "Who the hell are you, Panzer? Do you think you're Goodwin?" His eyes stopped at me a second on their way to Wolfe. To Wolfe he said, "It's you. It's always you."

A corner of Wolfe's mouth was up a thirty-second of an inch. For him a broad grin. He asked politely, "Does that mean something?"

"You know damn well—" Cramer bit it off. "Skip it. I don't want to interrupt. I have all day. Go right ahead. I might learn something."

"We haven't even started."

"*That* would be something. How you start."

"Well . . ." Wolfe shut his eyes. In ten seconds he opened them, looked at Saul, then at Fred, and then at Orrie. Then at me. "Get Mr. Abbott."

It didn't seem necessary to pretend I had to look up the number, so instead of going to my desk, where Cramer was, I went around to the other end of Wolfe's desk, reached for his phone, and dialed. It took four minutes to get the president of CAN—first an operator and then his secretary, and I had to say it was urgent. Since it was Wolfe's phone and I didn't go to mine, I heard only him.

"Good morning, Mr. Abbott. . . . Yes, I'm busy too, this won't take long. You said Monday evening that you have a warm and deep sympathy with Mrs. Odell and you want to oblige her; and this request is from her through me. I have just given three men the known facts about Mr. Odell's death. Their names are Saul Panzer, Fred Durkin, and Orrie Cather. They are experienced and competent. I ask you to give them permission to talk with people who are employed by your company— to move freely about the premises and talk with anyone who is available and willing. Only those who are willing. The police can do that without permission, but these men can't. They need a letter from you, and I want to send them to your office to get it. They will be considerate; they will not impose. They will not ask to talk with anyone who was here Monday evening. If you have a complaint about one of them, he will be withdrawn. May they come now for the letters? . . . No, of course not.

No compulsion. . . . No, there will be no difficulty about that. Inspector Cramer is here hearing me, and . . . Yes, Inspector Cramer of Homicide South. He is here in my office. . . . No, there is nothing official about this request. Mr. Cramer came to talk with me and interrupted my talk with these men. He has neither approved this request nor objected to it. . . ."

There was some more, mostly about interrupting people at work. When Wolfe hung up I was back in the red leather chair. He leaned back and sent his eyes to Fred and across Orrie to Saul. To them: "So you are going fishing. First to Mr. Abbott for credentials, and then scatter. As usual, anything whatever may or may not be significant. If any single question has precedence, it is who, if anyone, knew that Mr. Odell was going to that room and open that drawer. If you get no answer to that or any other question, you may at least get hints. Report to Archie daily as usual. I doubt if any bribing will be necessary or desirable, but the available funds are unlimited." He turned to me. "Five hundred?"

I said that should do for a start and went and opened the safe. From the supply in the cash box, always used bills, I got thirty twenties, sixty tens, and sixty fives, and split them three ways. Wolfe was telling them, "You heard me say that you will exclude those who were here Monday evening. Saul, you will try Dennis Copes. The question you want answered, did he know or think he knew that Kenneth Meer habitually inspected that drawer, is of course the one you won't ask. Orrie, you will try Dennis Copes's secretary if he has one. We want that question answered. Fred, you will follow your nose. Smile at people. Your smile is admirably deceptive. All of you, don't push and don't impose. There is no urgency.—Mr. Cramer. Have you a question or a comment before they go?"

Cramer said, "No," louder than necessary,

and with the used lettuce, distributed by me while Wolfe was talking, in their wallets, they got up and went. I gave Cramer a deceptive smile and said, "Let's trade," and he rose and crossed to the red leather chair and I took the one I belonged in.

Wolfe swiveled to face him. "Obviously," he said, "you are not in armor. Perhaps you will answer one question. Who told you about my Monday evening visitors?"

"Kenneth Meer. He phoned Lieutenant Rowcliff yesterday morning."

"Indeed."

"Yes." Cramer got a cigar from a pocket, stuck it in his mouth, and clamped his teeth on it. "You have Goodwin report verbatim, so I will. When Rowcliff told me about Meer's call, he said, 'Of course when they left, that fat son-of-a-bitch leaned back in his goddam tailor-made chair and shut his goddam beady eyes and worked his lips a while, and then he sat up and told that smart-ass Goodwin who the murderer was and told him to have him there at six o'clock when he came down from nursing his goddam orchids. So we'll put a man there to see who comes at six o'clock and then all we'll have to do is dig up the evidence and the motive.' Well, we did put a man there, and he reported that Theodore Falk came at half-past six. I thought it would save time and trouble to come and ask you, at least for the motive. That will help, getting the evidence."

Wolfe shook his head. "This isn't like you. Wasting your breath on clumsy sarcasm. And sitting here hearing me send those men on their errands you said nothing to them, or to me, about interference by private investigators in a murder case. How many times have you threatened to take my license? Are you desperate?"

"Yes."

"Oh." Wolfe's eyes opened wide. He shut them and opened them again. "Shall we have beer?"

"Yes."

Wolfe reached to the button to give Fritz the beer signal. Cramer took the cigar from his mouth, inspected the teeth marks, started it back toward his mouth, changed his mind, and laid it on the little table at his elbow. Fritz came with a bottle and glass on a tray and was told to bring another.

Cramer aimed a frown at me and then switched it to Wolfe. "I didn't come to ask for help. I'm not down that low. But it looks close to impossible. Of course lots of murder cases are impossible and have to be put on the open list, which means they're closed actually, but that won't do when the victim is a Peter Odell. But look at it. How can we get a murderer when we don't know who he wanted to kill? After three weeks we don't even know *that*. Durkin thinks we should have traced the bomb. Nuts. Seventeen people had a hand in getting the dope for that goddam program, and they have named nine sources that were contacted, and God knows how many others there were that they haven't named and won't name. And some of them learned enough to make their own bombs, and who did they tell? Of course we're still on that, but it looks worse now than it did a week ago."

He turned his palms up, the fingers spread. "You told them that the first question is who knew Odell was going to that room and open that drawer. Yeah? Sure. They'll bring you a list of names? Like hell they will. I don't suppose you already know who knew? That you told them that because I was here?"

"Nonsense. If I knew that, I probably wouldn't need those men."

Fritz had come with another bottle and glass, and Wolfe got the opener from the drawer and used it, and I got up and served Cramer. Wolfe poured, and as he waited for the foam to reach the right level, he told Cramer, "Of course you know *why* Odell went there and opened that drawer."

"I do?"

"Certainly. With a powerful drug in his pocket, opening the drawer where Browning kept his whisky? You are not a nincompoop."

"Naturally Mrs. Odell has told you."

"She told me that you showed her the LSD. I don't suppose it was flour or sugar, supplied by you. Why would you? Was it?"

"No." Cramer drank, emptied the glass, put it down on the table, picked up the bottle, and poured. He picked up the cigar, put it in his mouth, and took it out again. He looked at Wolfe, whose head was tilted back to drink, and waited for Wolfe's eyes to meet his.

"Why I came," he said. "Not to ask for help, but I thought it was possible that an exchange might help both of us. We have collected a lot of facts, thousands of facts, some established and some not. Mrs. Odell has certainly told you things that she hasn't told us, and maybe some of the others have too. We might trade. Of course it would hurt. You would be crossing your client, and I would be giving you official information that is supposed to be withheld. You don't want to and neither do I. But I'm making a straight offer on the square. I haven't asked you if this is being recorded."

"It isn't."

"Good." He picked up his glass. "That's why I came."

Wolfe swiveled, not his chair, his head, to look at me. The look said, as plain as words, "I hope you're appreciating this," and my look said, "I am." He turned back to Cramer and said, just stating a fact, "It won't do, Mr. Cramer."

"It won't?"

"No. There is mutual respect between you and me, but not mutual trust. If I gave you every word spoken to me by Mrs. Odell, and by the others, you would think it possible, even probable, that I omitted something. You say you have thousands of facts. If you gave me ten thousand, I would think it likely that you had reserved at least one. You know as well as I do that in the long record of man's make-believe, there is no sillier formula than the old legal phrase, 'the truth, the whole truth, and nothing but the truth.' Pfui."

"So you *would* omit something."

"Perhaps. I could add that if I did give you every word, you would know nothing helpful that you don't know now, but you wouldn't believe me."

"You're damn right I wouldn't." He looked at the glass in his hand and squinted at it as if he wondered how it got there. "Thanks for the beer." He put the glass, not empty, on the table, saw the cigar, and picked it up. I expected him to throw it at my wastebasket and miss as usual, but he stuck it in the beer glass, the chewed end down. He stood up. "I had a question, I had one question, but I'm not going to ask it. By God, you had the nerve—those men—with me sitting here—" He turned and walked out.

I didn't go to see him out, but when I heard the front door open and close, I went to the hall to see that he *was* out. Back in, I went to the safe to enter the outlay in the petty cash book. I don't like to leave things hanging. As I headed for my desk, Wolfe said, "I thought I knew that man. Why did he come?"

"He said he's desperate."

"But he isn't. So healthy an ego isn't capable of despair."

I sat. "He wanted to look at you. Of course he knew you wouldn't play along on his cockeyed offer. He thinks he can tell when you've got a good hand, and maybe he can."

"Do *you* think he can? Can you?"

"I'd better not answer that, not right now. We've got a job on. Am I to just sit here and take calls from the help?"

"No. You are to seduce either Miss Lugos or Miss Venner. Which one?"

I raised one brow. He can't do that. "Why not both?"

We discussed it.

10

*W*hen I had a chance, after lunch, I looked up "seduced" in the dictionary. "1. To persuade (one) as into disobedience, disloyalty, or desertion of a lord or cause. 2. To lead or draw (one) aside or astray, as into an evil, foolish, or disastrous course or action from that which is good, wise, etc; as to be *seduced* into war; to *seduce* one from his duty; to tempt or entice; as, pleasures that *seduced* her from home. 3. To induce to evil; to corrupt, specif., to induce to surrender chastity; to debauch."

Even on the 3 I couldn't charge him at some appropriate moment with having asked me to go too far, since we had no evidence that either of them had any chastity to surrender.

The best spot in the metropolitan area at four o'clock on a Saturday afternoon in June is an upper box at Shea Stadium, but I wasn't there that Saturday. I was sitting in the cockpit of a thirty-foot boat, removing a flounder the size of my open hand from the hook at the end of Sylvia Venner's line. The object I enjoy most removing from a hook is a sixteen-inch rainbow or Dolly Varden or cutthroat, but there aren't any in Long Island Sound. We had spent a couple of hours trying for stripers or blues without a bite and had settled for salmon eggs on little hooks. The name of the boat was *Happygolucky.* I had borrowed it from a man named Sopko, who had once paid Wolfe $7,372.40, including expenses, for getting his son out of a deep hole he had stumbled into.

It was from Sylvia Venner herself, on the telephone Wednesday afternoon, that I had learned that she didn't care for baseball, didn't like dancing, had seen all the shows in town, and wouldn't enjoy dining at Rusterman's because she was on a diet. The idea of a boat had come from her. She said that she loved catching fish, all except actually touching one, but the soonest she could make it was Saturday.

In fifty-six hours Saul and Fred and Orrie had produced nothing that would need help from me during the weekend. Friday evening I assembled the score for the two and a half days on a page of my notebook and got this:

> *Number of CAN employes who thought*
> *or guessed or hinted*
> —*that Odell was putting the bomb in the*
> *drawer to get Browning*   *4*
> —*that Browning planted the bomb to get*
> *Odell and somehow got Odell to go and*
> *open the drawer*   *1*
> —*that Dennis Copes planted it to get*
> *Kenneth Meer*   *2*
> —*that no one had planted it; the bomb*
> *was a left-over from the research for*
> *the program and was supposed to be*
> *de-activated*   *2*
> —*that Sylvia Venner had planted it to*
> *get Browning*   *1*
> —*that Helen Lugos had planted it to get*
> *Kenneth Meer*   *2*
> —*that Kenneth Meer had planted it to get*
> *Helen Lugos*   *1*
> —*that some kind of activist had planted*
> *it to get just anybody*   *3*

*—that it would never be known who had
planted it for whom*   **8**

If you skipped that I don't blame you; I include it only because I didn't want to waste the
time I spent compiling it. It adds up to twenty-
four, and they spoke with a total of about a
hundred people, so some seventy or eighty were
keeping their thinking or guessing or hinting to
themselves. Wolfe and I agreed, Friday evening,
to ignore the favorite guess. The idea that Odell
had himself supplied the bomb was out. His wife
would have known about it, and she would not
have given Wolfe a hundred grand to start dig-
ging. Also why the LSD in his pocket? Because he
was on the stuff and had it with him in case his
nerves needed a boost? Cramer and the DA had
certainly included that in their tries and had
chucked it. So no. Out. One of the four who liked
it was Dennis Copes, but that didn't prove anything. Saul's description of Copes was "5 feet 9,
160 pounds, brown hair down to his collar, sideburns that needed trimming, showy shirt and tie,
neat plain gray Hickey-Freeman suit, soft low-
pitched voice, nervous hands." He had chatted
with him twice and learned nothing useful. Of
course he hadn't asked if he knew or thought he
knew that Kenneth Meer had the habit of checking
on the whisky in the drawer, and though he is as
good as Wolfe at the trick of getting an answer
to an unasked question, it hadn't worked with
Copes.

Actually nothing worked with anybody. I have
just looked over my notes, and since there is nothing in them that helped us they certainly wouldn't
help you.

At four o'clock Saturday afternoon it looked
as if I wasn't going to get anything helpful from
Sylvia Venner either. She had stopped bothering
about the dimples. In blue shorts and a white

sleeveless shirt with big blue plastic buttons she was showing plenty of nice smooth skin with a medium tan, and her well-arranged face was the kind that looks even better in bright outdoor light than inside. While we were eating the broiled chicken supplied by Fritz, and yogurt and thin little tasteless crackers supplied by her, and pickles and raw carrots and celery, and she was drinking something called Four-Root Juice and I was drinking milk, she had suddenly said, "I suppose you know what etymology is."

"Hah," I said. "I work for Nero Wolfe."

"Why," she said, "is that relevant?"

"Certainly. He knows more words than Shakespeare knew."

"Oh. I don't really know anything about him except what he does. They tried to get him on my program once, but he wouldn't, so I didn't have to research him. Are you up on words too?"

"Not really. Just enough to get along on."

"I think words are fascinating. I was thinking, looking at you while you were dropping the anchor, take words like 'pecker' and 'prick.' In their vulgar sense, or maybe I should say their colloquial sense."

Without batting an eye I said, "You mean 'prick' as a noun. Not as a verb."

She nodded. "Yes, a noun. It means 'a pointed instrument.' 'Pecker' means 'an instrument for pecking,' and 'peck' means 'to strike repeatedly and often with a pointed instrument.' So the definition of 'pecker' and 'prick' is identical."

"Sure. I've never looked them up, but evidently you have."

"Of course. In Webster and in the OED. There's an OED at the office. Of course the point is that—well, well, there's a pun. 'Point.' The point is that they both begin with p, and 'penis' begins with p."

"I'll be damned. It certainly does."

"Yes. I think that may be relevant to that old saying, 'Watch your p's and q's.' *But*. But two other words, 'piss' and 'pee'—*p*-double-*e*—they start with *p* too. What it is, it's male chauvinism."

"I'm not sure I get that."

She sipped Four-Root Juice. "It's obvious. Women urinate too. So they have to call it 'piss' or 'pee' just because 'penis' begins with *p*. What if they called it 'viss' or 'vee,' and they made men call it 'viss' or 'vee' too? Would men like that?"

"Viss," I said. "Vee. I don't . . ." I considered it, sipping milk. "Oh. Vagina."

"Certainly. Virgin too, but that may be just coincidence."

"I admit it's a point. A voint. You may not believe this, but personally I wouldn't object. It even appeals to me. 'Excuse me while I viss.' 'Turn your back while I vee.' I rather like the sound of it."

"I don't believe it, and anyway not many men would. It's male chauvinism. And another point, 'poker' begins with a *p* too. Why didn't they make it 'poker' instead of 'pecker'? Because a poker is three feet long!"

"It is not. I've never seen a poker three feet long. More like two feet. Possibly thirty inches."

"You're just quibbling. Even two feet." She put her open hands out, apparently she thought two feet apart, but it was about twenty-eight inches. She picked up a pickle. Vickle. "So they couldn't very well call it 'poker.' Take another letter, take *f*. 'Female' begins with *f*. What is one of men's favorite four-letter colloquial words that begins with *f*?"

"Offhand I couldn't say. I'd have to think."

"All right, think."

So there I was, on a borrowed boat on Long Island Sound, alone with a Women's Libberette who was majoring in etymology. If you think that in the above exchange she was making a roundabout approach to a pass at me, I appreciate the compliment, but I doubt it. If so, my reaction cooled it. Even in such an ideal situation as a boat with a cabin at anchor in smooth water, I refuse to be seduced by quotations from Webster and the Oxford English Dictionary.

She was not a nitwit. Soon after we got our lines out she said, "What are you waiting for? You haven't asked me a single question about the murder."

"What murder?"

"Oh, come off it. Do you think I think my dimples took you?"

"No. I have never seen better dimples, and there's nothing wrong with other parts of you either, but a newspaperman I know thinks you planted the bomb to get Browning, and I wanted to get a close-up of you. With a good look and some talk with a woman, I can tell if she is a murderer. The way they eat helps too. For instance, do they lick their fingers."

She was frowning at me. "Do you really—no, of course you don't. All right, I'll play. Have you decided about me?"

"Not to cross you off, but ten to one you didn't plant the bomb. But three to one, make it five to one, you have a pretty good idea who did. You've been there four years, you know everybody, and you're smart."

"I am not smart. If I was smart I would have hooked that skunk Browning instead of letting Helen Lugos take him. Do you know who I could love?"

"No, but I'd like to."

"All right, I'll tell you. I could love the man who can prove I'm not dumb. I simply can't persuade myself I'm not dumb. Browning is going to be it, he's going to be the top cock, and where will I be? No, I didn't plant the bomb, but I could have."

"Who did?"

"I don't—*now* what have I done?"

She had snarled her line. Not purposely, to change the subject, because half an hour later, after we had unsnarled her and quit on stripers and were trying for blues, she said, "I've got a pretty good idea who might have. The bomb. But not for any signed statement. They always want signed statements. I'm not *that* dumb."

I made a cast. "Not me. I just want an idea to play with."

"Play? My god, you should have seen that room. Browning's office. When I got there Helen Lugos and Ken Meer were trying to keep people out. Ken's hands were bloody. When I heard what had happened—that was later—my first idea was that Ken had done it."

"How did he know Odell would come and open—"

"Not Odell. Browning. To kill Browning. Of course he—"

"Isn't Meer with Browning? His right hand?"

"Yes, but he hates him. No, that's wrong, it's not hate, it's—what, jealousy? It's worse than jealousy. It kills him that Helen does it with Browning. He got an itch for Helen when she came, two years ago, and he's got it bad. I've seen him look at her with that sick look—you know?"

I nodded. "Male chauvinism upside down."

"What? Oh. It is at that. But I dropped that idea. Ken certainly wants Helen, but he wants to move up even more, and if Browning was president he would be in a very good spot. So I still think he probably planted the bomb, but not for Browning, for Odell. So Odell couldn't be president. He knew Odell was going to come and open that drawer."

"How did he know that?"

"You'll have to ask *him*. I can't wrap it up for

you." She had her line in and squared around for another cast.

By the time the slant of the sun and my watch agreed that it was time to head for the marina, I had got all the questions in but had nothing to light a fire with. She doubted if Dennis Copes was involved because he was the hippie type and hippies aren't really headed anywhere, they just key up—according to her, not me. I know a hippie who tried—but he's not in this. She didn't know if Copes knew or thought he knew that Kenneth Meer inspected that drawer every day. She doubted if anybody inspected the drawer besides Browning himself, but if anyone did it was probably Helen Lugos; inspecting drawers is routine for secretaries. She had herself inspected it once, out of curiosity, about three years ago. Yes, it was twelve-year-old Ten-Mile Creek.

The Heron was in the parking lot at the marina and I drove Sylvia—sure, we had been Sylvia and Archie the last three hours—to a human hive in the East Seventies, only a block away from a spot where an FBI man had once insulted me because I was tailing a man he wanted to tail. She didn't invite me up. Wolfe was in the middle of dinner when I got home and he doesn't like to dawdle while I catch up, so I ate in the kitchen, with Fritz.

Later, in the office, when I asked him if he wanted Sylvia Venner verbatim he said yes, omitting only trivia, we had all evening. I asked, including the personal parts, and he said, enough of it to exhibit her. So I had a free hand. Omitting trivia, it took only ten minutes to get us on board the boat and under way, and another five to get us to the spot where we anchored and agreed that the air made us hungry. Of course I enjoyed my description of the picnic lunch in detail, but he didn't. He set his jaw and squinted at me, and did something he seldom does; he used profanity. "Good god," he growled. "Are you—how do you feel?"

"All right now. Of course it was tough, but what the hell, I was working. During the feast she said she supposed I knew what etymology is, and I said hah, I work for Nero Wolfe. She asked if that was relevant and said she didn't know much about him, that they tried to get him on her program but he wouldn't. You remember that."

"Yes."

"She said, quote, 'I think words are fascinating. Take words like "pecker" and "prick." In their vulgar sense, or maybe I should say their colloquial sense.' "

"Me: 'You mean "prick" as a noun, not as a verb.' "

"She: 'Yes, a noun. It means "a pointed instrument." "Pecker" just means "an instrument for pecking," and "peck" means "to strike repeatedly and often with a pointed instrument." So the definition of "pecker" and "prick" is identical.' "

"Me: 'Sure. I've never looked them up, but evidently—' "

His grunt stopped me. He growled, "I said omit trivia."

"This is not trivia. She was leading up to a point, and she made it. The point was that men make women say 'piss' and 'pee'—p-double-e—when they urinate because 'penis' begins with p, and what if *they* made *them* say 'viss' and 'vee'? Vagina. And she said it's male chauvinism. Doesn't that exhibit her?"

And once again I got a completely different reaction from the one I expected. I suppose I will never know him as well as I think I do. I did know where he stood on the question of male chauvinism, but I should have considered how he felt about words.

He said, "Indeed."

I said, "Yes indeed. Women's Lib."

He flipped a hand. "That's merely the herd syndrome. Fad. The issue is the influence of male dominance on language. Has that woman made a contribution to the study of linguistics? If so, there should be some indication in the record of matriarchy, but there is no adequate . . ."

Letting it hang, he pushed his chair back, rose, went straight to a spot in the shelves, got a book, and returned. As he sat, my good eyes told me it was *History of Human Marriage* by Westermarck. I had given it a ten-minute try one empty day long ago and decided I could get along without it. As he opened it, I asked, "Shall I tell the squad not to come in the morning because the issue now is a matter of linguistics, or will you need them for research?"

He glared at me, transferred it to the book, tossed it on the desk, and said, "Very well, proceed, but only what is material. No flummery."

So I no longer had a free hand. I reported. When I finished and he asked for comments, as usual, I said, "Nothing to raise my pay. One, I doubt if she is saving anything that would open a crack. Two, it would suit her fine if Browning dropped dead, but if she planted the bomb she wouldn't have risked a whole afternoon with me. She's not that kind. Three, at least we know that Meer had blood on his hands that other people could see, so maybe that helps to explain *him*."

"Not enough to justify that outrageous meal," he said, and reached for the book.

Fritz had left to spend a night and a day and another night as he saw fit, so before I went upstairs to dress properly for joining Lily Rowan's party at the Flamingo, I brought a bottle of beer to help with the language problem.

11

Since Wolfe's nine-to-eleven session in the plant rooms doesn't apply on Sundays, he was in the office when the help came at ten o'clock. That was about the most useless two hours we ever spent with them. Wolfe's idea was to have them talk about everyone they had seen, in the slim hope of our getting at least a glimmer of some kind of a hint.

No. Nothing.

If you are inclined to quit because I seem to be getting nowhere, no wonder. I'm sorry, but in these reports I don't put in stunts to jazz it up, I just report. Of course I can leave things out, and I do. I'll skip that two-hour Sunday conference, except for one little item. Orrie said that Dennis Copes didn't have a secretary, and the girl in the stenographer pool who often took stuff for him was a stuck-up bitch, and he added, "Of course Archie would have had her holding hands." He can't quite ditch the idea that he should have my job. I admit there is one little detail of detective work that he can do better than I can, but he doesn't know what it is so I won't name it. They were told to go back in the morning and try some more. The theory was that somebody there must know *something*, which seemed reasonable.

The only thing that happened that day worth

reporting was that Lily Rowan and I, at Shea Stadium, watched the Mets take the Cardinals, 7 to 3.

At ten o'clock Monday morning I sent a messenger to the CAN building with a white cardboard box addressed to Miss Helen Lugos. The box contained a cluster of Broughtonia sanguinea. They had been picked by Wolfe, who won't let even me cut his orchids, but the card in the box had my name. At 11:30 I decided that she must have opened it, phoned, and got a female who said that Miss Lugos was engaged and did I wish to leave a message. When you get up to vice-president, especially one who will soon be president because the other candidate was murdered, even secretaries are often hard to get. I decided that she might not have seen the box yet and postponed it to after lunch.

It was after four o'clock and Wolfe was up in the plant rooms when I finally got her. She said right off, "Thank you for the beautiful flowers." Neither warm nor cool, just polite.

"You're welcome. I suggested them, Mr. Wolfe picked them, and we both packed them. It's a bribe. Mr. Wolfe thinks I understand women better than he does and wants me to have a talk with you. I don't think this office is the best place for it because that's too much like telling you to come to a—oh, the District Attorney's office. I can come to your place, or we can meet anywhere you say, or we can share a meal in the little pink room at Rusterman's. Perhaps dinner this evening? Women are supposed to like pink rooms, as of course you know. I'm going on talking to give you time to consider it; I didn't suppose you'd have a yes right at the tip of your tongue."

"I haven't got one anywhere. Thank you, but no."

"Then the pink room is out. Have you a suggestion?"

"I have a question. Has Mrs. Odell asked *you* to talk with me?"

"Mrs. Odell hasn't asked *me* anything. She has hired Nero Wolfe to do a job, and she has asked people at CAN to cooperate, from Mr. Abbott down, as you know. We would like to suit their convenience. In this case, *your* convenience."

"Mrs. Odell didn't hire you, she hired Nero Wolfe."

"I work for him."

"I know you do. And I work for Mr. Browning. When he wants to talk with someone, he doesn't expect them to be willing to talk with me instead. If Mr. Wolfe wants to talk with me, all right, I suppose I'll have to. At his office, of course. When does he want me to come?"

There was no point in prolonging it. I said distinctly, "At six o'clock today. An hour and a half from now."

She said distinctly, "Very well, I'll be there," and hung up.

I went to the kitchen, poured myself a glass of milk, and told Fritz, "I'm done. Washed up. I've lost my touch. I'm a has-been. You knew me when."

He was at the big table doing something to a duckling. "Now, Archie," he said. "He told me about that woman's diet when I took his breakfast up this morning, but you ate a good lunch. What else has happened?"

"Another woman. She spit at me just now. Spat. On the phone."

"Then *she* is washed up, not you. You are looking at the wrong side. Just turn it over, that's all you ever have to do, just turn it over."

"I'll be damned." I stared at him. "You sound like a guru."

There was no telling what would happen if Wolfe came down at six o'clock and found an unexpected female sitting in the red leather chair—

or rather, there *was*—so when the glass of milk was down I went up three flights, entered, walked down the aisles between the rainbow benches of the three rooms—cool, medium, and warm—and opened the door of the potting room. He and Theodore were at the long bench, making labels. I stopped halfway across and said, "I'm not breaking a rule. Emergency. We have wasted forty dollars' worth of orchids."

He waited until I stopped to turn his head. "She's not available?"

"Oh, she's available, but not for menials. When she dies—the sooner, the better—and ascends, she won't waste her breath on Saint Peter, she'll speak only to Him, with a capital H. She'll be here at six o'clock to speak to You, with a capital Y. I apologize and will expect a pay cut."

"Pfui. I agree that you have not broken a rule." He made a face. "I'll be prompt."

On the way out I stopped to apologize to the two pots of Broughtonia sanguinea. On the way down, I decided that the milk needed help and went to the kitchen for a tall glass of gin and tonic with a sprig of mint and a dash of lime juice. Also for Fritz. I needed friendly companionship.

I was supposing she would be strictly punctual, maybe even a couple of minutes early, but no. She *was* female. She came at 6:18, in a peach-colored blouse with long sleeves and a brownish skirt, narrow, down to a couple of inches below her knees, and she talked to me. She said, "I'm sorry I'm a little late." Not being in a mood to meet her halfway, I said, "So am I."

Wolfe had not told me how he intended to proceed, though he had come down from the plant rooms on the dot at six o'clock, and though he often asks my advice on how to handle a woman and sometimes even follows it. He soon showed me, and her, that this time he needed no help with his game plan. As she got to the red leather chair, he said, "Good afternoon, Miss Lugos. Thank you for coming," and when she was seated and had her ankles crossed and her skirt tugged, he rose, crossed almost to the door, turned, and said, "I have an errand to do in the kitchen. My agent, Mr. Goodwin, will ask you some questions on behalf of Mrs. Odell."

He went.

"I'm as surprised as you are," I told her, "but it's just like him. No consideration for other people. I think I told you that he thinks I understand women better than he does. He actually believes that. So here we are, in a private detective's office which could be bugged, instead of the pink room at Rusterman's. If you like something wet after a day's work, name it and we may have it."

Her lips were twitching a little. "I ought to get up and go," she said. "But I suppose—that would only—"

"Yes," I agreed, "it would only. Anyway, you've flubbed it. On the phone you stiff-armed me. You put me in my place. But if you really meant it, you would have sent the orchids back, or even brought them. Unless you dropped them in the wastebasket?"

She flushed and her lips tightened. I believe I have mentioned that her face was different from any two angles, and it was different flushed. With most faces that you enjoy looking at, you know exactly why, but not with her kind. Flushed, it was again quite different, and I approved of that too. Then suddenly it became another face entirely. She laughed, with her mouth open and her head back, and I think I grinned with pleasure. I really did.

"All right, Mr. Goodwin," she said, "you win. I *didn't* drop them in the wastebasket. They're in a vase. I almost wish we were at Rusterman's. But as you said, here we are. So ask your questions."

96

I had erased the grin. "Would you like a drink?"

"No, thank you."

"Then let's see. First, I guess, that evening you heard what those people said, six of them, when Mr. Wolfe asked them where they were that weekend. Were they all telling the truth?"

"I don't know. How could I?"

"You might. Maybe you have heard Browning say something that shows he wasn't on a boat from Friday afternoon to Sunday afternoon, or maybe Kenneth Meer has said something that shows he wasn't hiking in Vermont. From your look I think you think I'm a damn fool to suppose you would tell me things like that. But I'm not. In an investigation like this only a damn fool would expect a full and honest answer to any question he asks anybody, but he asks them. For instance, the question I ask you now. This: Did Dennis Copes know that Kenneth Meer looked in that drawer every day to check on the whisky supply?"

"That's a trick question. It assumes that Kenneth Meer did look in the drawer every day."

"So it does. All right, did he?"

"No. As far as I know, he didn't. Mr. Browning checked on the whisky supply himself."

"Did he buy it himself?"

"He buys it by the case. It's sent to his home and he brings it, two bottles at a time."

"Does Kenneth Meer drink bourbon?"

"I don't think so. He drinks vodka."

"Do you drink bourbon?"

"Very seldom. I don't drink much of anything."

"Did *you* look in the drawer every day to check on the whisky supply?"

"No. Mr. Browning did the looking himself."

"I thought secretaries checked everything."

"Well—that's what you thought."

"You know Dennis Copes."

"Certainly."

"Two people think he might have planted the bomb to get Meer because he wants Meer's job. If so, he might have thought Meer looked in the drawer every day. Have you any idea why he might think that?"

"No. I have no idea why he thinks anything."

"One person thinks that Kenneth Meer planted the bomb to get Browning because you go to bed with him. Have you any idea about that?"

"Yes, I have. It's absurd."

"A newspaperman I know doesn't think it's absurd. Of course it's really three ideas. One, that you are intimate with Browning, two, that Meer knows it and can't stand it, and three, that he planted the bomb. Are they all absurd?"

She wasn't visibly reacting. No flush on her skin, no flash in her eyes. She said, with no change in pitch, "The police have asked me about this. My relations with Mr. Browning are my business and his. Certainly not yours. Women do go to bed with men, so it may not be absurd for people to think I am intimate with Amory Browning, but the idea that Kenneth Meer tried to kill him, *that's* absurd. Kenneth Meer has big ideas about his future. He thinks he's headed for the top, and he's counting on Amory Browning to help him along."

"But you're there. What if he wants you more than anything else? This *is* my business, Miss Lugos. The police think it's theirs, too, you just said so. It's not absurd to think a man's desire for a woman can be so hot that no other desire counts. There have been cases."

"Kenneth Meer isn't one of them. You don't know him, but I do. How much longer is this going to take?"

"I don't know. It depends. Not as long as it would with Mr. Wolfe. He likes to ask questions that seem to be just to pass the time, but I try to stick to the point. For instance, when Mr. Wolfe asked you that evening if you thought the person who put the bomb in the drawer was here in the room, you said you had no idea, but naturally you would say that, with them here. What would you say now, not for quotation?"

"I would say exactly the same, I have no idea. Mr. Goodwin, I—I'm tired. I'd like some—some whisky?"

"Sure. Scotch, bourbon, rye, Irish. Water, soda, ice."

"Just whisky. Any kind—bourbon. It doesn't matter."

She wasn't tired. The fingers of both hands, in her lap, had been curling and uncurling. She was tight. I mean tense, taut. As I went to the kitchen and put a bottle of bourbon—not Ten-Mile Creek —and a glass and a pitcher of water on a tray, I was trying to decide if it was just the strain of discussing her personal affairs with a mere agent, or something even touchier. I still hadn't decided when I had put the tray on the little table by her chair and was back at my desk. She poured about two fingers, downed it with three swallows, made a face and swallowed nothing a couple of times, poured half a glass of water, and swallowed that.

"I told you—" she began, didn't like how it sounded or felt, and started over. "I told you I don't drink much."

I nodded. "I can bring some milk, but it's an antidote for whisky."

"No, thank you." She swallowed nothing again.

"Okay. You said you have no idea who put the bomb in the drawer."

"Yes, I haven't."

I got my notebook and pen. "For this, since this room is *not* bugged, I'll have to make notes. I have to know where you were every minute of that day, that Tuesday, May 20. It was four weeks ago, four weeks tomorrow, but it shouldn't strain your memory, since the police of course asked you that day or the day after. Anyone going to Browning's room went through your room, so we'll have to do the whole day, from the time you arrived. Around ten o'clock?"

"There was another door to his room."

"But not often used except by him?"

"Not often, but sometimes it was. I'm not going to do this. I don't think you have a right to expect me to."

"I have no *right* to expect anything. But Mr. Wolfe can't do the job Mrs. Odell hired him to do unless he can get answers to the essential questions, and this is certainly one of them. One reason I say that is that Kenneth Meer told a newspaperman that anyone who wanted to know how it happened should concentrate on Helen Lugos. Why did Meer say that?"

"I don't believe it." She was staring at me, which made her face different again. "I don't believe he said that."

"But he did. It's a fact, Miss Lugos."

"To a newspaperman?"

"Yes. I won't tell you his name, but if I have to, I can produce him and he can tell you. He wasn't a stranger to Meer. They were choir boys together at St. Andrew's. When he tried to get Meer to go on, Meer clammed. I'm not assuming that when you tell me how and where you spent that day, I'll know why Meer said that, since you'll tell me exactly what you told the police and evidently it didn't help them any, but I must have it because that's how a detective is supposed to detect. You got to work at ten o'clock?"

She said no, nine-thirty.

Even with my personal and private shorthand it filled more than four pages of my notebook. The timing was perfect. It was exactly 7:30 when we had her in the file room and the sound and shake

100

of the explosion came, and Fritz stepped in to reach for the doorknob. So it was time to eat. If I am in the office with company, and Wolfe isn't, when dinner's ready, Fritz comes and shuts the office door. That notifies me that food is ready to serve, and also it keeps the sound of voices from annoying Wolfe in the dining room across the hall, if I have to continue the conversation.

That time I didn't have to, and I didn't want to. I wanted to consider a couple of the things she had said without her sitting there with her face, and I wanted my share of the ducklings with mushrooms and wild rice and wine while it was hot from the oven. It's one of the dishes Wolfe and Fritz have made up together, and they call it American duckling on account of the wild rice, and I'm for it.

So I said she was tired, and she said yes, she was, and got up, and I thanked her, and thanked her again as I opened the front door to let her out.

Of course I didn't mention her as I joined Wolfe at the dining table. He had one of the ducklings carved, so that would have been talking business during a meal, which is not done. But when we had finished and moved to the office and Fritz had brought coffee, he showed that the week of marking time was getting on his nerves by demanding, "Well?" before I had lifted my cup.

"No," I said.

"Nothing at all?"

"Nothing for me. For you, I can't say. I never can. You want it verbatim, of course."

"Yes."

I gave it to him, complete, up to the details of her day on Tuesday, May 20. For that I used the notebook. As usual, he just listened; no interruptions, no questions. He is the best listener I know. When I finished, the coffee pot and our cups were empty and Fritz had come for them.

I put the notebook in the drawer. "So for me,
101

nothing. Of course she didn't open the bag and shake it, who does? She knows or suspects something that may or may not be true and might or might not help, and to guess what it is needs a better guesser than me. I don't think she planted the bomb. She wasn't there at her desk in the next room when it went off, which was lucky for her, but she says she often went to the file room for something, nearly always when Browning wasn't in his room. Of course the cops have checked that. Also of course it was a waste of time to have her name the seventeen people she saw go into Browning's room. The bomb wasn't put in the drawer while Browning was there unless he did it himself, and there's another door to his room. As for who entered his room when he wasn't there, there was a total of nearly two hours when *she* wasn't there, according to her. As for her reason that Kenneth Meer wouldn't want to kill Browning, toss a coin. You'd have to use a lie detector on Meer himself."

He grunted. "Miss Venner, and now Miss Lugos."

"Meaning I should have seduced at least one of them. Fire me."

"Pfui. I complain of your conduct only directly, never by innuendo. You offend only deliberately, never by shortcoming. Miss Lugos did not plant the bomb?"

"One will get you ten."

"Does she know who did?"

"No bet. She could think she knows. Or not."

"Confound it." He got up and went to the shelves for a book.

12

Six days later, at noon Sunday, June 22, the five of us sat in the office and looked at each other. Saul and Fred and Orrie and I looked at Wolfe, and he looked back, his eyes moving, not his head, from me past Orrie and Fred to Saul in the red leather chair.

"No," he said. "This is preposterous. Amphigoric. And insupportable." He looked at me. "How much altogether, including you?"

I shut my eyes and in less than half a minute opened them. "Say three thousand dollars. A little more."

"It will be a deduction on my tax return. Call Mrs. Odell and tell her I am quitting. Draw a check to her for the full amount of the retainer."

Fred and Orrie had to turn their heads to look at me. Saul, in the red leather chair, didn't have to turn his head. I looked at Wolfe, especially the left corner of his mouth, to see how bad it was.

Plenty of things had happened. There had been three thunderstorms in a row Wednesday afternoon. Jill Cather, Orrie's wife, had threatened to walk out on him because he didn't get home until five in the morning Tuesday after taking a CAN female researcher to dinner and a show, though he explained that the meal and the tickets had been paid for by the client. The West Side Highway, northbound, had been closed for repairs all day Friday. Fred Durkin, tailing a CAN male employee Thursday evening, had lost him, and he hates to lose a tail; and on Friday, Elaine, his oldest daughter, had admitted she was smoking grass. Saul Panzer had spent two days and a night at Montauk Point trying to find a bomb maker, and drawn a blank. On Friday the Labor Department announced that the Consumer Price Index had gone up .3 of one percent in May. A busy week.

Personally I had done wonders. I had answered at least a hundred phone calls, including dozens from the three helpers. They were *trying* to help. Also including three from Mrs. Odell. I had discussed the situation for about an hour with a member of the CAN news staff, brought by Orrie. His real reason for coming had been to have a chat with Nero Wolfe. I had spent an evening with Sylvia Venner and a male chauvinist friend of hers, also a CAN employee, at her apartment. I had washed my hands and face every day. I could go on, but that's enough to show you that I was fully occupied.

Wolfe hadn't been idle either. When Inspector Cramer had rung the doorbell at eleven-thirty Friday morning, he had told me to admit him, and he had held up his end of a twenty-minute conversation. Cramer had no chips on his shoulder. What brought him was the fact that Cass R. Abbott, the president of CAN, had come to see Wolfe the day before, a little after six o'clock, and stayed a full hour. Evidently Cramer had the old brownstone under surveillance, and if so, he positively was desperate in spite of his healthy ego. He probably thought that Abbott's coming indicated that Wolfe had a fire lit, and if so, he wanted to warm his hands. I think when he left, he was satisfied that we were as empty as he was, but with those two you never know.

What Abbott's coming actually indicated was

that the strain was getting on his nerves, and for a man so high up that would not do. When he got parked in the red leather chair, he told Wolfe he would like to speak with him confidentially, and when Wolfe said he could, there would be no recording, Abbott looked at me, then back to Wolfe, and said, "Privately."

Wolfe shook his head. "Professionally nothing is reserved between Mr. Goodwin and me. If he leaves the room and you tell me anything relevant to the job we are doing—trying to do—I would tell him, withholding nothing."

"Well." Abbott ran his fingers through his mop of fine, white hair. "I have had a check on you but not on Goodwin. You hold up, but does he?"

"If he doesn't, I don't. What good is a chain with a bad link?"

Abbott nodded. "A good line. Who said it?"

"I did. The thought is not new, no thought is, but said better."

"You use words, don't you?"

"Yes. On occasion, in six languages, which is a mere smattering. I would like to be able to communicate with any man alive. As it is, even you and I find it difficult. Are you sure you can prevent my getting more or less than you want me to from what you tell me or ask me?"

Abbott's raised eyebrows made his long, pale face look even longer. "By god, I can try."

"Go ahead."

"When I say 'confidential,' I mean you will not repeat to Mrs. Odell anything I say about her."

Wolfe nodded. "See? You don't mean that. Of course I would repeat it if it would serve my purpose or her interest to do so. She has hired me. If you mean I am not to tell her your name, I am to give her no hint of who said it, yes. —Archie?"

"Right," I said. "Noted and filed."

"Then that's understood," Abbott said. He slid further back in the chair, which is deep. "I have known Mrs. Odell twenty years. I suppose you know she is a large stockholder in the Continental Air Network. I know her very well, and I knew him well—her husband. That's one point. Another point is that I have been president of CAN for nine years, and I'm retiring in a few weeks, and I don't want to leave in an atmosphere of distrust and doubt and suspicion. Not distrust or suspicion of me, not of anyone in particular, it's just in the air. It pervades the whole damn place, the whole organization. To leave when it's like that—it would look like I'm getting out from under."

He hit the chair arm with a fist. *"This goddam murder has got to be cleared up!* You probably wondered why I let you turn those three men loose in my building to go anywhere and see anyone. I did it because the police and the District Attorney were completely stumped, they were getting absolutely nowhere, and I thought you might. One reason I thought you might was that there was a good chance that Mrs. Odell had told you things that she hadn't told them. But that was a week ago, a week yesterday, and where have *you* got to?"

"Here." Wolfe patted his desk blotter. "I'm always here."

"Hell, I know you are. Do you know who put that bomb in that drawer? Have you even got a good guess?"

"Yes. You did. You thought they were going to choose Mr. Browning, and you favored Mr. Odell."

"Sure. All you need is proof. As I thought, you have done no better than the police, and you have had ten days. Last evening I discussed the situation with three of my directors, and as a result I phoned this morning to make the appointment. I am prepared to make a proposal with the backing of my Board. I suppose Mrs. Odell has paid you a retainer. If you will withdraw and return her retainer, we will reimburse you for all expenses you have incurred, and we will engage you to investigate the death of Peter Odell on behalf of the corporation, with a retainer in the same amount as Mrs. Odell's. Or possibly more."

I had of course been looking at him. Now I looked at Wolfe. Since he was facing Abbott, he was in profile to me, but I had enough of his right eye to see what I call his slow-motion take. The eye closed, but so slow I couldn't see the motion of the lid. At least twenty seconds. He certainly wasn't giving Abbott a long wink, so the other eye was collaborating. They stayed shut about another twenty seconds, then opened in one, and he spoke. "It's obvious, of course. It's transparent."

"Transparent? It's direct."

"It is indeed. You have concluded that Mr. Odell himself supplied the bomb, intending it for Mr. Browning, and mishandled it. And that Mrs. Odell hired me, not to discover and disclose the truth, but to impede its disclosure and prevent it if possible. You assume that either she is hoodwinking me or she has been candid with me. If the former, you decry my sagacity; if the latter, your proposal invites me to betray a trust. A waste of time, both yours and mine. I would have thought—"

"You're taking it wrong. It's not—you're twisting it. We merely think that if you were acting for the corpor—"

"Nonsense. Don't persist. I am neither a ninny nor a blackguard. Under a strain you and your colleagues have lost your wits. There is the possibility that you want to pay me to contrive some kind of skulduggery for you, but I doubt if you have misjudged me to that extreme. If you have, don't bother. Don't try floundering. Just go."

Abbott did not get up and go. He had to take it that he wasn't going to get what he had come for, but he stuck for another half an hour, trying to find out what we had done or hadn't done and what we expected to do. He found out exactly nothing, and so did Wolfe.

When I went back to the office after letting Abbott out, Wolfe glared at me and muttered, "Part of his proposal is worth considering. Returning the retainer."

He considered it for two days and three nights. In the office at noon Sunday, after another two-hour session with us—as I reported six pages back—he told me to call Mrs. Odell and tell her he was quitting and to draw a check to her for the full amount of the retainer; and Saul and Fred and Orrie looked at me and I looked at Wolfe, especially the left corner of his mouth, to see how bad it was.

It was bad all right, it was final, but I did not reach for the phone. "Okay," I said. "Since I started it, I admit I should be the one to finish it, but not with a phone call. I'd rather finish it the way I started it, face to face with her, and to do it right I should take the check and hand it to her instead of mailing it. No deduction for expenses?"

"No. The full amount. Very well, take it."

If we had been alone I might have tried discussing it, but with them there it was hopeless. Discussion would have to be with her, and then with him maybe. I went and got the checkbook from the safe, filled out the stub, tore the check out, and swung the typewriter around. I type all checks. That was the first one I had ever drawn for an even hundred grand, and with all the 0's it was a nice round figure. I took it to Wolfe and he signed it and handed it back. As I took it, Saul said, "I've asked so many people so many questions the last ten days, it's a habit, and I'd like to ask one more. How much is it?"

Even from Saul that was a mouthful, and my eyes opened at him. But Wolfe merely said, "Show it to him. Them."

I did so, and *their* eyes opened, and Saul said, "For her that's petty cash, she's really loaded. Sometimes you ask us for suggestions, and I'd like to make one. Or just another question. Instead of returning it to her, why not offer it to someone who needs it? A two-column ad in the *Times* and the *Gazette* with a heading like COULD YOU USE A HUNDRED THOUSAND DOLLARS? Then, 'I'll pay that amount in cash to the person who gives me information that will satisfactorily identify the person responsible for the death of Peter Odell by the explosion of a bomb on May twentieth.' Your name at the bottom. Of course the wording would—"

Wolfe's "No" stopped him. He repeated it. "No. I will not make a public appeal for someone to do my job for me."

"You have," Saul said. "You have advertised for help twice that I know of."

"For an answer to a particular question. Specific knowledge on a specified point. Not a frantic squawk to be pulled out of a mudhole. No."

So when they left a few minutes later, they weren't expected back. By noon Monday Fred and Orrie would be on chores for Bascom or some other outfit, and Saul too if he felt like it.

As for me, my chore wouldn't wait—or I didn't want it to. As someone said, probably Shakespeare, " 'twere better done," and so forth. Of course a person such as a Mrs. Peter Odell would ordinarily not be in town on a June Sunday, but she would be. She was ignoring weekends, and from a phone call by her Saturday morning she knew there would be a Sunday conference. So I rang her and asked if I could come at five o'clock, because earlier she would probably have the television on and I didn't want to share her attention with Cleon Jones at bat or Tom Seaver on the mound.

Wolfe had gone to the kitchen. For Sunday lunch with Fritz away he usually does something simple like eggs *au beurre noir* and a beet and watercress salad, but that time it was going to be larded shad roe casserole with anchovy butter and parsley and chervil and shallots and marjoram and black pepper and cream and bay leaf and onion and butter. It would take a lot of tasting, and he can taste. I went to the kitchen to tell him Mrs. Odell would see me at five o'clock, and he nodded, and I mounted the two flights to my room.

That was a busy four hours; shaving and changing from the skin out, going down for my third of the shad roe, which we ate in the kitchen, looking at the telecast from Montreal—where the Mets were playing the Expos—on the color set, which, like everything else in my room, was bought and paid for by me, and writing. Not on the typewriter, because when I'm being particular, I do better longhand, and that had to be done right. When I went downstairs a little before four-thirty, the third draft was in my pocket, with the check. Wolfe was up in the plant rooms and I buzzed him on the house phone to tell him I was leaving.

Since parking shouldn't be a problem Sunday afternoon, I went to the garage for the Heron, crossed town on Thirty-fourth, and turned uptown on Park. Driving in midtown Manhattan can still be a pleasure—from two to eight A.M. and a couple of hours on Sunday. There was actually a gap at the curb on Sixty-third Street between Fifth and Madison. The LPS man at the entrance to the stone mansion was not the same one, and this one had better manners; he said thank you when he returned my card case. Inside I was ushered to the elevator by the same woman in a neat gray uniform and was told to push the button with a 4.

In the upper hall, the client's voice came through the open door to the big room, "In here!"

She was on the oversized couch, one leg on it straight and the other one dangling over the edge, with sections of the Sunday *Times* scattered around. The television was not on—but of course the game was over. As I crossed to her she said, "You'd better have something. You certainly don't on the telephone."

"We got careless once when our phone was tapped and we're leery. I don't suppose it's tapped now, but once was enough. Yes, I have something." I got the check from my pocket. "I thought I should bring it instead of mailing it."

She took it, frowned at it, frowned at me, again at the check, and back at me. "What's the idea?"

"Mr. Wolfe is bowing out. Quite a bow, since he has spent more than three thousand dollars. Three thousand dollars in twelve days and we haven't got a smell. One reason I'm bringing it instead of mailing it, I wanted to tell you that that's all there is to it, he's simply pulling out. He thinks it shows strength of character to admit he's licked. I can't see it and don't intend to, but I'm not a genius."

She surprised me. Up to that moment she had given me no reason to suppose that the arrangements inside her skull were any better than average, but she had reached a conclusion before I finished. Her eyes showed it, and she said it, with a question: "How much did Browning pay him?"

"Uh-huh," I said, and turned a chair to face her, and sat. "You would, naturally. If I talked for five hours, giving cases, I *might* be able to convince you that he couldn't possibly double-cross a client, on account of his opinion of himself, but I think there's a shorter way. I've told you on the phone about the three men we have called in to help. They were there this morning when he said

111

it was hopeless and he was quitting. When he told me to draw a check to return the retainer, Saul Panzer suggested that instead of returning it, he might put an ad in the *Times* saying that he would pay it to anyone who would give him information that would identify the murderer, and Mr. Wolfe said no, he would not make a frantic squawk to be pulled out of a mudhole. That was—"

"Of course! He *would* say that!"

"Please hold it, I've just started. So I drew the check and he signed it, and I phoned you. But I think I can prove that he didn't sell out, and I want to try. I think I can get him to tear the check up and go on with the job, with your help. May I use your typewriter?"

"What for? I don't believe it."

"You will. You'll have to." I got up and crossed to a desk, the one with a typewriter on an extension. As I pulled the chair out and sat, I asked where I would find paper and she said, "The top drawer, but you're not fooling me," and I said, "Wait and see," and got out paper and a sheet of carbon.

She preferred not to wait. As I got the third draft from my pocket and spread it out on the desk, she kicked the sections of the *Times* aside, left the couch, and came and stood at my elbow, and I hit the keys. I didn't hurry because I wanted it clean. No exing. As I pulled it out, I said, "I had to type it here because he might recognize it from my machine, and this is going to be your idea." I handed her the original and gave the carbon a look:

NERO WOLFE HAS $50,000

in cash, given to him by me. He will pay it, on my behalf, to any person or persons who supply information to him that leads to the conclusive identification of the man or woman who placed a bomb in a drawer of the desk of Amory Browning on Tuesday, May 20th, resulting in the death of my husband.

The information is to be given directly to Nero Wolfe, who will use it on my behalf, and the person or persons supplying it will do so under these conditions:

1. All decisions regarding the significance and value of any item of information will be made solely by Nero Wolfe and will be final.

2. The total amount paid will be $50,-000. If more than one person supplies useful information, the determination of their relative value and of the distribution of the $50,000 will be made solely by Nero Wolfe and will be final.

3. Any person who communicates with Nero Wolfe or his agent as a result of this advertisement thereby agrees to the above conditions.

"With your name at the bottom," I said. "A reproduction of your signature, Madeline Odell, like on your check, and below it 'Mrs. Peter J. Odell' in parenthesis, as usual, printed. Now hear this. Of course he'll know I wrote it, but if he thinks I wrote it at home and brought it, he'll balk. No go. As I said, that's why I didn't type it there. It has to be your idea, suggested by you after I told you about his reaction to Saul Panzer's suggestion. He may phone you. If he does, you'll have to do it right. Then of course the question will be, what will happen? I think it will work, and certainly it *may* work. It's ten to one that someone knows something that would crack it open, and fifty grand is a lot of bait."

I was on my feet. "So if you'll sign it, the original, and keep the carbon, and I'll need two samples of your signature on plain paper, one for the *Times* and one for the *Gazette*, to make cuts."

"You're pretty good," she said.

"I try hard. Whence all but me have fled."

"What?"

"The burning deck."

"What burning deck?"

"You don't read the right poems." I swiveled the chair. "Sit here? That pen is stingy, I tried it. Mine's better."

"So is the one on my desk." She moved, went to the other desk, which was bigger, and sat. "I'm not convinced, you know. This could be an act. You can phone to say it didn't work."

"If I do, it won't be an act, it will be because he is pigheaded. I mean strong-minded. It will depend on you if he phones."

"Well." She reached for the pen in an elegant jade stand. "*I* have a suggestion. It shouldn't be fifty thousand. Figures like that, fifty thousand or a hundred thousand, they don't hit. In-between figures are better, like sixty-five thousand or eighty-five."

"Right. Absolutely. Change it. Make it sixty-five. Just draw a line through the fifty thousand."

She tried the pen on a scratch pad. I always do.

13

*I*t worked.

Driving downtown and across to the garage on Tenth Avenue, I considered the approach. Over the years I suppose I have told Wolfe 10,000 bare-faced lies, or, if you prefer in-between figures, make it 8,392, either on personal matters that were none of his business or on business details that couldn't hurt and might help, but I have no desire to break a world record, and anyway the point was to make it stick if possible. I decided on a flank attack and then to play it by ear.

When I entered the office at 6:22, he was at his desk working on the Double-Crostic in the *Times*, and of course I didn't interrupt. I took my jacket off and draped it on the back of my chair, loosened my tie, went to the safe and got the checkbook and took it to my desk, and got interested in the stubs for the month of June. *That* was a flank attack all right. In a few minutes, maybe eight, he looked up and frowned at me and asked, "What's the balance now?"

"It depends," I said. I twisted around to get Exhibit A from my jacket pocket and rose and handed it across. He read it, taking his time, dropped it on the desk, narrowed his eyes at me, and said, "Grrr."

"She changed the fifty to sixty-five herself,"

I said. "That heading could have been Archie Goodwin has sixty-five thousand instead of Nero Wolfe. She didn't actually suggest it, but she thinks I'm pretty good. She said so. When I told her you were quitting and handed her the check, she said. 'How much did Browning pay him?' I told her that if I talked for five hours I might be able to convince her that you wouldn't double-cross a client, but actually I doubt it. You may not give a damn what she thinks of my employer, but I do. I brought her to you. She said things and I said things, and when it became evident that nothing else would convince her, I went to a typewriter and wrote that. I don't claim the wording is perfect. I am not Norman Mailer."

"Bah. That peacock? That blowhard?"

"All right, make it Hemingway."

"There was a typewriter there?"

"Sure. It was the big room on the fourth floor where apparently she does everything but eat and sleep. As you see, the paper is a twenty-pound bond at least half rag. Yours is only twenty percent rag."

He gave it a look, a good look, and I made a note to pat myself on the back for not doing it on my typewriter. "I admit," I said, "that I didn't try to talk her out of it. I certainly did not. In discussing it I told her that I thought it would work, that it's ten to one that someone knows something that would crack it open, and that fifty grand is a lot of bait. That was before she changed it to sixty-five. This is a long answer to your question, What's the balance? As I said, it depends. I brought the check back, but it would only cost eight cents to mail it. If we do, the balance will be a little under six thousand dollars. There was the June fifteenth income tax payment. I'm not badgering you, I'm just answering your question. But I'll permit myself to mention that this way it would not be a frantic squawk for someone to pull you out of a mudhole. I will also mention that if I phone her that the ad—correction, advertisement—has been placed, she will mail another check. For sixty-five thousand. She would make it a million if it would help. As of now nothing else on earth matters to her."

What he did was typical, absolutely him. He didn't say "Very well" or "Tear the check up" or even "Confound it." He picked the thing up, read it slowly, scowling at it, put it to one side under a paper weight, said "I'm doing some smoked sturgeon Muscovite. Please bring a bottle of Madeira from the cellar," and picked up the Double-Crostic.

14

*t*he ad was on page 6 of the *Times* Tuesday morning and page 9 of the *Gazette* that afternoon —two columns, bold face, with plenty of space all around—and two more conditions had been added:

1. *The $65,000 may all be paid to one person, or it may be divided among two or more people.*
2. *The $65,000 or any part of it will be paid only for information, not for a suggestion, conjecture, or theory.*

The other conditions, with only three words changed, followed.

We had discussed a certain probability and decided nothing could be done about it. Would Homicide South see the ad? Sure. Would they keep an eye, several eyes, on our front door to see who came? Sure again. Then what? They would horn in on our investigation of a murder. They would try to get for nothing what our client had offered $65,000 for. They would probably even put a tap on our phone, and the scientists have done such wonders for mankind that you can no longer tell whether your wire has been tapped or not. I admit science works both ways; we intended to record all conversations with callers, either in person or by phone. Also, with the bank balance fat again, we had reserves ready. Saul and Fred and Orrie were back, and at two P.M. Tuesday they were in the front room playing pinochle.

The very first one was wild. There had been four phone calls, but they had all been obvious screwballs. The first one in the flesh rang the doorbell a little before three o'clock. Through the oneway glass panel in the front door, he looked like a screwball too, but I opened the door and he handed me a card—a small blue card with a name on it in fancy dark blue letters: Nasir ibn Bekr. Okay, a foreign screwball, but I let him in. He was slim and wiry, he came about up to my chin, his hair and face and eyes were all very dark, and his nose would have gone with a man twice his size. On that warm June day his jacket was buttoned and the collar of his blue shirt was limp. When I turned after closing the door, he handed me a piece of paper, the ad clipped from the *Times*, and said, "I will see Mr. Nero Wolfe."

"Perhaps," I said. "He's busy. You have information?"

"I am not sure. I may have."

Not a screwball. Screwballs are sure. I asked him to wait, motioning to the bench, took the card to the office and handed it to Wolfe, and was told to bring him, but I didn't have to. He was there, right behind me. The big Keraghan in the office is thick, but there's no rug in the hall; he was the silent type. He should be closer to me than the red leather chair, so I blocked it off and motioned to the yellow one near the corner of my desk. Then I went and closed the door to the hall, for a reason. The arrangement was that when I admitted a visitor and intended to show him to the office, I would notify the trio by tapping on the door to the front room. When I had got the visitor to the office, I would close that door so that they would not be seen as they went down the hall to the alcove at the kitchen end, and they would take a look at the visitor through the peephole that was covered on the office side by a trick picture of a waterfall. They would also listen. As I crossed back to my desk, Nasir ibn Bekr said, "Of course this is being recorded," and I said, "Then I won't have to take notes."

Wolfe said, "The conditions in the advertisement are clear?"

He nodded. "Certainly. Perfectly clear. The information I have, it is my personal knowledge, but its worth is for you to determine. I must ask a question. We find nothing in your record to indicate clearly your position regarding the situation in the Near East. Are you anti-Zionist?"

"No."

He turned to me. "Are you?"

"No. My only objection to Jews is that one of them is as good a poker player as I am. Sometimes a little better."

He nodded. "They have learned how to use guile. They have had to." To Wolfe: "Perhaps you know that there are Arab terrorists—mostly Palestinians—active in this country, mostly in Washington and New York."

"It is said that there are, yes."

"It is not just said. There *are*. I am one." He unbuttoned the top button of his jacket, slipped his hand in, and brought out a small brown envelope. From it he got a folded paper. He rose to hand it to Wolfe, but terrorists are in my department and I moved fast enough to get a hand to it first. As I unfolded it, he sat and said. "That is the names of five men, but I am not sure it is their real names. It is the only names I know for them. We meet every week, once a week, on Sunday afternoon, in an apartment in Jackson Heights. That is the address and telephone number. Armad Qarmat lives there. I do not have addresses for the others. As you see, my name is not there. I have printed them because with names like ours that is better than writing."

I had given it a look and handed it to Wolfe.

"I see you have television," Nasir ibn Bekr said. "Perhaps you saw a program on CAN in May, May seventh, 'Oil and Mecca.'"

Wolfe shook his head. "I turn on the television rarely, only to confirm my opinion of it." Not having been asked, I didn't say that I had seen the "Oil and Mecca" program at Lily Rowan's.

"It was a full hour," the terrorist said. "It was partly a documentary in pictures of the production of oil in Arab countries, but it was also a commentary. It did not say that the existence and welfare of Israel were of more importance to civilization, and of course to democracy, than the Arabian oil, but it strongly implied that. It was definitely anti-Arabian and pro-Israel. That was a Wednesday. The following Sunday we discussed it, and we wrote a letter to CAN demanding a retraction of the lies it told. The next Sunday Armad said there had been no answer to the letter, and he had learned that the man responsible for the program was a vice-president of CAN named Amory Browning. That was Sunday, May eighteenth. We decided that it was an opportunity to take action against the anti-Arabian propaganda in this country."

His head turned to me and back to Wolfe. "I should explain that I became a member of the group only a year ago, not quite a year, and I am not yet completely in their confidence. Especially Armad Qarmat has not fully decided about me, and that is why I said I am not sure, I *may* have information. I do know they had three bombs, I saw them one day. In April. That Sunday, May eighteenth, one of them suggested using one of the bombs at the CAN office, and if possible the office of Amory Browning. There was some discussion, and I saw that Armad Qarmat stopped it on account of me. As I said, he has not fully accepted me. The next Sunday, May twenty-fifth, one of them spoke of the explosion of a bomb in Amory Browning's office, killing Peter Odell, another vice-president, but Armad Qarmat said that should not be discussed. Since then there have been four meetings, four Sundays, and the bomb has not been mentioned."

He tilted his head back and took a couple of breaths, then looked at me and back at Wolfe. "There," he said, "I have told you. This morning I saw your advertisement. Sixty-five thousand dollars is a great deal of money. It will be better if I am frank. At first I thought I would give you more . . . more detail. More that was said, as I am sure it must have been said, when I was not present. But then I saw it would be better to tell you exactly how it was, and that is what I have done. The advertisement does not say you require proof."

He slipped his hand inside his jacket, again produced the brown envelope, and took something from it. "In my position," he said, "I have to consider the possibilities. This is a piece of a dollar bill that I tore in half. If you find that what I have told you is the information you ask for in your advertisement, and if I do not come to claim the sixty-five thousand dollars, it may be because I can't. If I am dead, I can't. In that case someone else will come, and if so he will have the other half of the dollar bill. Will that be satisfactory?" He put the piece of the bill on Wolfe's desk, and I went and got it. It was a ragged tear. I handed it to Wolfe.

He cocked his head at the terrorist. "I suppose," he said, "you speak Arabic."

"Of course."

"Arabic is spoken at your Sunday meetings?"

"Of course."

"Fortunately. For you. Your attempt at

speaking English as it would be spoken by a cultured Palestinian is inept. You shouldn't try it. What is your real name?"

He didn't bat an eye. "That wouldn't help you," he said. Then he asked a question. To me the words he used were only sounds, but I knew it was a question by the inflection.

"I did," Wolfe said, "but long ago. Arabic is not one of my languages. I want your name because I may need to ask you something."

Nasir ibn Bekr shook his head. "I have told you all I know that could help. This is a big risk for me, coming to you at all, and I will not add to it. You are right, Arabic is not my native tongue. My native tongue is Spanish. But my Arabic is good; it must be. I will say this, if something happens, if one of them says something that you should know, I will telephone or come." He rose and buttoned the top button of his jacket, looked at me and back at Wolfe, and said, "I must thank you."

"A moment," Wolfe said. "This house is under surveillance. By the police. Mr. Goodwin will show you out—at the rear. There's a passage through to Thirty-fourth Street."

The terrorist shook his head. "That isn't necessary. Thank you again, but I can't be followed. No matter who tries, even in Baghdad or Cairo I can get loose."

He moved, and I went to open the door. It would have been mildly interesting to step out to the stoop and see who came out from where, to tail him, but I didn't want to give anyone the idea that we gave a damn. As I turned from shutting the front door, I called down the hall, "All clear!" and the trio appeared from the alcove and followed me into the office. They lined up at the end of Wolfe's desk.

"Comments," Wolfe said. "Fred?"

"I don't think so," Fred said. "How would he

get in Browning's room when no one was there, and why would he pick the bottom drawer?"

"Orrie?"

"The League of Jewish Patriots," Orrie said.

"No," Saul said, "he's not the type. They're all athletes. Of course he's a Jew, but not that kind. I agree with Fred. His reasons, and also the timing. The bomb doesn't have to be connected with the fact that that was the day they were going to decide on the new president, but it's hard to believe that it wasn't."

"But it's only ten to one," I said. "Even if it's twenty to one we have to give it a look."

"Actually," Wolfe said, "he is taking no risk. Even if he knows there is only one chance in a thousand, he is giving himself that chance to fill a purse.—Archie. Type this list of names, adding his name, and the address, and give it to Fred. Fred, you will see if it is worth an effort. Enter that apartment only with all possible precaution; it isn't worth even the slightest hazard. Our usual understanding, of course. Further comments?"

There weren't any. I swung the typewriter around, Fred sat, and Saul and Orrie went to the front room.

That's a sample of what the ad brought us. I don't say typical; it wasn't. Of course if you advertised in those two papers that you had sixty-five grand to hand out, no matter what for, and your name and address were in the phone book, you would know you would get plenty of calls and callers, and the best we could expect was that just one of them would really have something. If what I was after was merely to fill pages, it would be easy to add a dozen or so with the next couple of days, up to 9:42 P.M. Thursday evening. Some of the items might even add to your knowledge of human nature—for instance, the middle-aged man in a spotless white suit and a bushy wig who had had a dream Tuesday night. He came Wednesday afternoon. In the dream a man had opened the bottom drawer of a desk and fastened, with tape, a small plastic box to the partition above the drawer, about nine inches back from the front. A thin copper wire about a foot long protruded from the end of the box. With the drawer open only a couple of inches he had taped the loose end of the wire to the inside of the front of the drawer, and closed it, and departed. If we would show him photographs of the men who had entered or might have entered Amory Browning's room that day, he would tell us which one had put the box in the drawer, and he would so testify under oath. That was what made it really good, that he would testify without even being subpoenaed. Or the female star buff who phoned for an appointment and came Thursday morning—a skinny specimen with hollow cheeks and big dreamy eyes. If we would give her the birth dates of all the suspects she would supply information that would almost certainly do the trick.

There were three or four that Saul and Orrie spent some time and effort on. Fred had made no headway with the Arab terrorists.

To show you how low I was by Thursday evening after dinner, I'll admit what I was doing. First, what I wasn't doing. I was not at the poker table at Saul's apartment. I was in no mood for being sociable, and I would probably have drawn to an inside straight. I was at my desk in the office, scowling at the entries in a little looseleaf book which I call The Nero Wolfe Backlog. It contained a list of certain items that were in his safe deposit box at the Continental Trust Company, and I was considering which one or ones should be disposed of at the current market price if I was asked for a suggestion, as I would be soon if we got nothing better than Arab terrorists and dreamers and star buffs. Wolfe was at his desk with a book of stories by Turgenev, and that was bad too.

When he's low he always picks something that he has already read more than once.

When the doorbell rang, I glanced at my wrist watch as I rose, as usual. Sometimes it's needed for the record. Eighteen minutes to ten. I went to the hall, flipped the switch of the stoop light, took a look, stepped back in the office, and said, "You'll have to mark your place. It's Dennis Copes."

"You haven't seen Dennis Copes."

"No, but Saul described him."

He shut the book without using the bookmark, and of course no dog ear, since it was Turgenev. I went and opened the front door, and the visitor said, "You're Archie Goodwin," and stepped right in as if I wasn't there.

"And you're—" I said.

"Copes. Dennis Copes. Not as famous as you, but I will be. Is your famous fat boss available?"

I was so damn glad to see him, to see someone who might actually have something to bite on, that I thought that on him the long hair and two-inch sideburns looked just fine. And when, in the office, he marched across and put out a hand, Wolfe took it. He seldom shakes hands with anybody, and never with strangers. He *was* low. As Copes sat he hitched his pants legs up—the nervous hands Saul had mentioned.

"That was a good ad," he said. " 'Any person who communicates as a result of this advertisement thereby agrees to the above conditions.' Very neat. What agency?"

Wolfe frowned. "Agency?"

"Who wrote it?"

"Mr. Goodwin."

"Oh." He looked at me: "Nice going Archie." Back to Wolfe: "That ad would have made a wonderful five-minute spot—you and Mrs. Odell, you right here at your desk and her standing with her hand on your shoulder. You would do most of the talking, with your voice. She would have been glad to pay for prime time—say ten o'clock. A much bigger audience than the ad. Didn't you consider it?"

"No."

"Too bad. How many nibbles have you had?"

"None."

"*None?* Impossible. All right, you're not telling and why should you? But you can't say it's none of my damn business, because in a way it is. If someone else knows what I know, and if they've already told you, I've missed the bus. Have you— let's see, how shall I put it—has anyone told you anything that makes you want to have a talk with Kenneth Meer or Helen Lugos?"

Wolfe eyed him. "Mr. Copes. Mrs. Odell's advertisement asks for information *to* me, not *from* me. I'll say this: if I had received information that gave me reason to speak with Miss Lugos or Mr. Meer, I would have arranged to see them, and I haven't."

Copes nodded. "Fair enough. Now I have to admit something. I have to admit that I should have told the police what I'm going to tell you. I admit I'm not exactly proud of the reason *why* I didn't tell them. I admit it wasn't because of any love I have for Kenneth Meer or Helen Lugos; it was because it would have put me right in the thick of a damn nasty murder mess. All right, I admit that. With you it's different on two counts. One, you won't handle it like they would. You'll have more consideration for—well, for *me*. Two, if you get what I think you'll get, *I'll* get sixty-five thousand dollars and *can* I use it!"

The fingertips of his right hand were dancing a jig on the chair arm, and he turned the hand over and curled them. "Part of what I'm going to tell you probably won't be news to you. You probably know why Odell went to Browning's room and opened that drawer. Don't you?"

Wolfe grunted. "Do you?"

"Yes. He was going to put LSD in the whisky bottle so Browning would bobble it at the directors' meeting or not even be there. You probably know that, from Mrs. Odell. I'm going to tell you how *I* know it. How I *knew* it. I knew it the day before, that he was going to. I knew it on Monday, May nineteenth."

"Indeed."

"Yes. Of course you know there were two doors to Browning's room—one from the anteroom, Helen Lugos's room, and one from the hall. And here's another thing I have to admit, another reason I haven't told the police: that Monday afternoon I entered Browning's room by the door from the hall when I knew he wasn't there. It was right after lunch, and I—"

"Wasn't that door locked?"

"Not always. When Browning left by that door to go down the hall to the rear, he usually pushed the button on the lock so he could go back in without using his key. I wanted to look at something I knew was on his desk, and I knew he wasn't there, so I tried that door and it opened. I didn't make any noise because I didn't want to be interrupted by Helen Lugos, and the door to her room was half open, and I could hear voices—hers and Kenneth Meer's. Mostly his. I suppose this is being recorded."

"Yes."

"Of course. What isn't?" He took a notebook from his pocket and opened it. "So I'd better read it. The first thing I heard him say—he said, 'No, I'm not going to tell you how I found out. That doesn't matter anyway, I *did* find out. Odell is going to dope that bottle of whisky with LSD tomorrow afternoon, or he thinks he is, and I want to be damn sure you don't open the drawer to take a look at the usual time. Don't open it any time after lunch. Don't open it at all, don't go near it, because—well, *don't.*' And she said, 'But Ken, you'll have to tell me—Wait. I'd better make sure—' And there was the sound of her pushing her chair back."

The fingertips were at it again, this time on his knee. "So I got out quick. She was probably going to come to make sure there was no one in Browning's room. I hadn't got to the desk, I was only a couple of steps from the door—I had left it open a crack—and I got out fast. I didn't go back to my room because there's another man in it with me and I wanted to be alone, so I went to the men's room and sat on the john to think it over. Of course what I wanted to do, I wanted to tell Browning. Maybe Meer was going to tell him but from what he said it didn't sound like it. But I didn't want to tell Browning I had entered his room by the hall door—of course I didn't. And I didn't know what Meer intended to do. I knew he intended to do something since he had told her not to go near the drawer, but what? What would *you* have thought he intended to do?"

Wolfe shook his head. "I don't know him. You did."

"Sure, I knew him, but not well enough for that. For instance, I thought he might wait until about four o'clock Tuesday and then take the bottle from the drawer and put another bottle in its place, and have the whisky analyzed and have the bottle checked for fingerprints. He knew Browning never took a drink until about half past four or a quarter to five, when the program scripts had all been okayed. I considered all the possibilities, what *I* could do, and the one thing I *had* to do was make sure that Browning didn't drink any doped whisky. So I decided to be there in the room with him Tuesday when he okayed the last script—I usually was—and when he got the bottle out, I would say that there was nothing Odell wouldn't do to get the president's job, and it might be a good idea to open the other bottle. There was always another bottle there, unopened, often two."

129

"You knew that," Wolfe said.

"Sure, several of us did. Often a couple of us were there when he opened the drawer. One thing I considered: tell Browning that I had heard Meer say that to Helen, but not that I had been in his room. But that would have been very tricky because where was I and where were they? You may know that a lot of people think I want Meer's job."

"That has been said, yes."

"Maybe I do and maybe I don't. I want to get on, sure, who doesn't, but it doesn't have to be *his* job. Anyway, I had to consider that too. Of course if I had known what Meer was going to do, if I had even suspected it, I would have gone straight to Browning and told him just like it was. I didn't and of course I regret it."

"You're assuming that Meer had decided to put a bomb in the drawer?"

"Certainly. My God, don't I have to? *Didn't* I have to?"

"You made that assumption that day—the next day? When you learned what had happened?"

"I certainly did."

"Five weeks ago. Five weeks and two days. What have you done to verify it?"

Copes nodded. "It's easy to ask that. What *could* I have done? Could I ask people if they had seen Meer with a bomb? Could I ask them if they had seen him go into Browning's room? Could I ask Helen Lugos *anything*? Could I hire a detective? Naturally you're thinking I may have cooked this up. Of course you are. You'd be a damn fool if you didn't. But there's one detail, one fact, that you have to consider. As I said, you probably knew that Odell went there to put LSD in the whisky because Mrs. Odell probably told you, but how did I know? One thing, Odell must have had the LSD with him, but there has been no mention of it. It could be that the police are reserving it, or it could be that he had it in his hand when he opened the drawer

130

and no traces of it have been found, but I doubt that because they are very thorough and very expert on that kind of thing. Probably they're keeping it back. Maybe you know?"

Wolfe skipped it. "That's a detail, yes. Not conclusive, but indicative. You're aware, Mr. Copes, that without support your information is worthless. If I challenge Mr. Meer or Miss Lugos by telling them what you have told me and they say you lie, what then? Have you a suggestion?"

"No. The ad didn't say I have to tell you how to *use* the information. You're Nero Wolfe, the great detective; I'm just a guy who happened to hear something. Of course I realize Browning will have to know I entered his room that way, that will have to come out, maybe even on the witness stand. You've got it now on tape. If it costs me my job I'll need that sixty-five thousand. Should I tell Browning myself? Now?"

"No." Wolfe made it positive. "Tell nobody anything. May I see that notebook?"

"Certainly." He took it from his pocket and got up to hand it over. It was loose-leaf with little rings. Wolfe gave several pages a look and stopped at one.

"Did you write this that day? Monday?"

"No. I wrote it the next day, Tuesday evening, after the—after what happened. But that's exactly what he said. I can swear to it."

"You may have to." Wolfe handed the notebook back to him. "I can't tell you how I'll proceed, Mr. Copes, because I don't know. If I need you, I'll know where to find you." He leaned back, his head against the chair back, and shut his eyes. I honestly don't know if he realizes that that's no way to end a conversation. I do.

15

Saul and Fred and Orrie and I are still discussing what Wolfe said that Friday morning—or rather, what we *didn't* say.

They came at ten o'clock and I played it back for them twice—the tape of the talk with Dennis Copes—and we considered two angles: one, Was it straight or had he hatched it to get Meer? and two, If it was straight, how were we going to wrap it up? By eleven o'clock, when Wolfe came down from the plant rooms, we hadn't got very far with either one. He told us good morning, put a raceme of Dendrobium chrysotoxum in the vase on his desk, sat and sent his eyes around, and asked, "Have you a program?"

"Sure," I said. "Just what you're expecting, ask you for instructions."

"One thing," Saul said. "He comes first. How good is it?"

"Obviously. On that he said one thing that was strikingly suggestive. Have you considered it?"

We looked at one another. "Well," Saul said, "that line about him being just a guy who happened to hear something. We agree that that sounds good. If he's faking it that's *very* good. A wonderful line."

Wolfe shook his head. "I mean something

quite different. One specific thing he said that suggests a possible answer to all questions. You haven't considered it?"

"We considered everything," I said. "What specific thing?"

He shook his head again. "Not now. Even if it means what it *may* mean, we must first decide about him. The detail which—as he said—we have to consider: if he didn't learn about the LSD as he says he did, then how? Of course you have discussed that. And?"

"And nothing," Orrie said. "We've talked with a lot of people these two weeks, and not the slightest hint of the LSD angle from anyone. You told us to keep that good and tight and we did."

I said, "The only mention of it we have heard has been from Mrs. Odell and Falk, and he got it from her. Possibly he also got it from his cousin who is an assistant DA, but he didn't say so. Apparently it *is* tight. Abbott evidently thinks Odell had a bomb in his pocket, not LSD."

Wolfe nodded. "We'll have to explore the possibilities. Orrie. You will try again with the CAN personnel, this time on the one question, could his knowledge of the LSD have come through anyone there? He need not have learned it a month or even a week ago; even yesterday would do. Take care not to divulge it yourself. Fred. Forget the Palestinians. You are on speaking terms with members of the police force. A dozen?"

"Only two in Homicide," Fred said.

"That may be enough. Knowledge of the LSD may not be limited to the Homicide men. The first to arrive at the scene may have found it. You need not take pains to reserve our knowledge of it; Mr. Cramer knows that we know about it. Does one of them know Mr. Copes or anyone connected with him?—Saul. You will try the other possible source, Mrs. Odell and Miss Haber. I doubt if Mrs. Odell has mentioned it to anyone whatever, but

Miss Haber procured the LSD for her, and Mr. Copes would have needed to know only that to make a plausible conjecture. Does Mr. Copes know anyone she knows and might have told? Probably you should try from his end, not hers, but that's for you to decide. Have enough cash with you. If there is any urgent need for help, Archie will be here."

Wolfe's eyes went to Fred, to Orrie, and back to Saul. "We want this, messieurs. If you find another probable source for Mr. Copes's knowledge of the LSD, it will be more than satisfactory. Ironically, it will probably get him sixty-five thousand dollars for supplying the required information. I wish you luck."

As Saul stood he said, "I have a question. Might it help if we knew what he said that was strikingly suggestive? Could it hurt?"

"Yes, it could hurt. It could divert your interest. I shouldn't have mentioned it. My tendency to strut. Display, like diffidence, is commendable only when it avails. Ignore it."

Just fine. What else could they do? Not to mention me. So when they were gone, I ignored it. I sat and ignored it while he glanced through the little stack of mail I had put on his desk, and when he looked up I asked, "Do I do anything while I am being here?"

"Yes," he said. "This is Friday."

"Right."

"I would like to see Miss Lugos and Mr. Meer, not together. And not today. It's possible that today or this evening we'll get something. Miss Lugos at eleven o'clock tomorrow and Mr. Meer at three?"

"It's a June weekend and it may take pressure. I'm not objecting, I'm just asking. I would enjoy pressing somebody. Anybody."

"So would I."

I got at the phone and dialed.

16

*t*hat afternoon Orrie and I had a two-piece argument, first on the phone and then face-to-face. Around three o'clock he called to say he would be working the whole weekend because he was taking a female CAN researcher to Atlantic City. I asked if he wished to leave a message for Jill, his wife, in case she called, and he said she was in Tokyo, which was plausible since she was an airline hostess. I said he would be paid to six P.M. Friday, and he said he would come and discuss it. He came a little after four, knowing that Wolfe would be up in the plant rooms, and said it would be a working weekend and he should also get twenty cents a mile for the use of his car; he might get something useful from her and he was certainly going to try. I said okay, eight hours Saturday and eight Sunday, he couldn't expect to be paid for the time he spent in bed, and he said bed was the best place to get really confidential, and I had to agree. But not eight dollars an hour for fifty-two hours, and not the hotel bill. He said Mrs. Odell had a billion, and I said not more than a hundred million even with inflation, and we should leave her something for groceries. We finally settled on a lump sum to cover everything, $364.00, which was seven dollars an hour. I may as well mention now that the client got exactly nothing for that little expense item.

By eleven o'clock Saturday morning, when Helen Lugos came, Fred had also drawn a blank. He had talked with five city employees he knew, one of them a sergeant in Homicide, and none of them had had any contact with Dennis Copes or had any information about him. He doubted if any of them knew about the LSD, but of course they might be keeping the lid on. He was proceeding.

Saul had collected a bag of facts about Copes —where and how he lived, his habits, his friends, his background, his personal finances—but nothing that gave us any pointers, so they wouldn't give you any either, and I'll skip them. He had found no connection whatever with Mrs. Odell or Charlotte Haber, but was preparing an approach to Charlotte's kid brother, since there had been a hint that it was on account of him that she had known how to get the LSD.

Helen Lugos not only wasn't late this time, she was ten minutes early, so she was stuck with a mere agent again until Wolfe came down from the plant rooms. She wanted to know what was so urgent that she had to change her weekend plans, and I explained that I only obeyed orders.

Wolfe entered, told me good morning first and then her, put the flowers for the day in the vase and arranged them so he would have the best view, swiveled his chair to face her, and sat.

"I don't thank you for coming," he said. "I'm not disposed to thank you for anything. I have reason to believe that you are withholding information that would be of value. Indeed, I think you have lied. Don't bother to deny it. I tell you that only to establish the temper of the conversation. I'll be trying to find support for my opinion. What will you be doing?"

She would be staring. She *was* staring. "I

know what I *ought* to be doing," she said. "Leaving. I ought to be on my way out."

"But you're not. You wouldn't, even if I'm wrong, because you want to know why. That's what makes us the unique animal, we want to know why and try to find out. We even try to discover why we want to know why, though of course we never will. It's possible that upon consideration you have concluded, or at least suspected, that you may have made a mistake or two. For instance, nineteen days ago, a Monday evening, I asked you if you thought it likely that the person who put the bomb in the drawer was present in this room and you said you had no idea. 'None at all,' you said. And twelve days ago, again a Monday, when you were alone with Mr. Goodwin and he asked what you would say if he asked that question, you replied that you would say exactly the same, you had no idea. I'll try once more. What would you say now?"

"My god," she said. "How many times . . ."

"What would you say now?"

"The same!"

Wolfe nodded. "You should know, Miss Lugos, that this is being recorded electronically. The recorder is on a closet shelf in the kitchen, so that a man there can change the tape if necessary. I now have a special reason for wanting to learn beyond question the nature of your relations with Kenneth Meer. What you tell me will be tested thoroughly by wide inquiry. So?"

"It has already been tested by the police." Her chin was up and a muscle in the side of her neck was twitching, barely perceptible even by good eyes. "We're not—we're associated in our work because we have to be. Personally we don't —we are not close."

"But he would like to be?"

"He thinks he—yes."

"Do you read books?"

She did what everybody does when asked an unexpected and irrelevant question. Her eyes widened and her lips parted. For two seconds exactly the same as if he had asked her if she ate cats. Then she said, "Why—yes. I read books."

"Do you read much fiction?"

"I read *some*."

"Then you may be aware that most competent storytellers, even lesser ones, have an instinctive knowledge of the possibilities of human conduct. They often present two characters who have a strong mutual attachment in secret but who have other people believing that they are hostile. But not the reverse. Not two who have a mutual animus but have others believing that they like or love each other. Storytellers know it can't be done. So do I. I know I can't learn if you and Mr. Meer are in fact close by asking you questions and watching your face as you answer them, so I won't try. I know it's futile for me to ask you anything at all, but I wanted to see you again and hear you speak, and I would like to ask one specific question, more for what the question will tell you than for what the answer will tell me. Mr. Goodwin got your detailed account of your movements on that Tuesday, May twentieth. I would like one detail of the preceding day, Monday, May nineteenth. In the early afternoon, shortly after lunch, Mr. Meer was with you in your room. Tête-à-tête. What did you talk about? What was said?"

I won't say I actually enjoyed what happened next, but I appreciated being there to see it. Having seen him walk out on people I don't know how many times, say a hundred, it kind of evened up to see him once as the walkee instead of the walker. She didn't glare or clamp her jaw or spit, she just go up and went. I admit he didn't glare or spit either; he just sat and watched her go. I did too until she was out; then I stepped to the hall to see that she shut the front door. When I stepped back in, he was opening the drawer to get the bottle opener—so he had rung for beer.

"Tell me once more," I said, "that I understand women better than you do. It gives me confidence. But don't ask me to prove it. I said two weeks ago that she didn't open the bag and shake it. I also said she didn't plant the bomb, but now I don't know. Did Copes strikingly suggest that she did?"

"Confound Copes," he growled. "And nothing can be expected from Saul or Fred during the weekend."

He picked up the top item on the stack of the morning mail. It was a check from Mrs. Odell for $65,000.

17

Kenneth Meer was early too. When I answered the doorbell a little before three, I saw his car down at the curb, a dark green Jaguar. He had an oversized brief case, brown leather, under his arm, presumably to save the trouble of locking the car, and when I asked if he wanted to leave it on the hall bench, he said no and took it along to the office. I said before, when I first saw him, that his poorly designed face was tired too young, and now, as he sat in the red leather chair and blinked at Wolfe, his long, pointed nose above his wide square chin looked like an exclamation point with a long line crossing at the bottom instead of a dot.

He kept the brief case on his lap. "I resent this," he said. He sounded as peevish as he looked. "Why couldn't I come yesterday—last evening? Why today?"

Wolfe nodded. "I owe you an apology, Mr. Meer. You have it. I hoped to have by now definite information on a point I wanted to discuss with you, but it hasn't come. However, since you're here, we may as well consider another point. Your bloody hands. A week after the explosion of that bomb you were in distress, severe enough to take you to that clinic and then to me. Later, when I became professionally involved, the nature of your distress was of course of interest. There were various possibilities: You had yourself put the bomb in the drawer and the burden of guilt was too heavy for you. Or you hadn't, but you knew or suspected who had, and your conscience was galling you; your imagined bloody hands were insisting, *please pass the guilt*. Or merely the event itself had hit you too hard; the sight of the havoc and the actual blood on your hands had put you in shock. Those were all valid guesses, but Mr. Goodwin and I didn't bother to discuss them; we rarely waste time discussing guesses."

"I like that, *please pass the guilt*," Meer said. "I like that."

"So do I. Mr. Goodwin will too. He once said that I ride words bareback. But the devil of it is that after more than three weeks the guesses are still guesses, and it may possibly help to mention them to you. Have you a comment?"

"No."

"None at all?"

"No."

"Does the distress persist? Do you still get up in the middle of the night to wash your hands?"

"No."

"Then something that has been done or said must have removed the pressure, or at least eased it. What? Do you know?"

"No."

Wolfe shook his head. "I can't accept that. This morning I was blunt with Miss Lugos and told her I thought she was lying. Now I think you are. There is another point concerning you that I haven't broached that I'll mention now. Why did you tell a man that anyone who wanted to know how it happened should concentrate on Helen Lugos?"

Meer didn't frown or cock his head or even blink. He merely said, "I didn't."

Wolfe's head turned. "Archie?"

"You said it," I told Meer, "to Pete Damiano.

I can't name the day, but it was soon after it happened. About a month ago."

"Oh, him." He grinned, or make it that he probably thought he grinned. "Pete would say anything."

"That's witless," Wolfe said. "You knew it was likely, at least possible, that that would be remembered and you would be asked about it, and you should have had a plausible reply ready. Merely to deny it won't do. It's obvious that you're implicated, either by something you know or something you did, and you should be prepared to deal with contingencies. I am, and I believe one is imminent. I ask you the same question I asked Miss Lugos this morning, in the same terms: In the early afternoon of Monday, May nineteenth, shortly after lunch, you were with Miss Lugos in her room, tête-à-tête. What did you talk about? What was said?"

That got a frown. "You asked her that? What did she say?"

"What did *you* say?"

"Nothing. I don't remember."

"Pfui. I've asked you seven questions and got only no's and nothings. I've apologized to you; now I apologize to myself. Another time, Mr. Meer. Mr. Goodwin will show you out."

I rose, but stood, because Meer thought he was going to say something. His lips parted twice but closed again. He looked up at me, saw only an impassive mug, got up, tucked the brief case under his arm, and moved. I followed him, but got ahead in the hall, opened the front door, and waited until he was down and at the door of the Jaguar to close it. Back in the office, I asked, "Do we need to discuss any guesses?"

Wolfe grunted. "You might as well have gone before lunch. Shall I apologize to you?"

"No, thanks. The phone number is on your pad, as usual." I went and got my bag from the hall and let myself out, on my way to the garage for the Heron and then to the West Side Highway, headed for Lily Rowan's glade in Westchester. That's what she calls it, The Glade.

18

*A*mory Browning did something Monday morning that had never been done before. He walked down the aisles of the three plant rooms, clear to the potting room, without seeing an orchid. I didn't actually see him, since he was behind me, but I'm sure he did. With that blaze of color, right and left and overhead, you'd think he would have to be blind. In a way he was.

It was twenty past ten and I had just returned from a walk crosstown to the bank and back, to deposit the check from the client, when the ring of the doorbell took me to the hall, and there was the next president of CAN. When I went and opened the door, he crossed the sill and went on by and headed for the office, and when I got there he was standing at the end of Wolfe's desk.

"Where is he?" he demanded.

"Where he always is at this hour, up on the roof. He'll be down at eleven. You can wait, or maybe I can help."

"Get him down here. Now."

The man at the top speaking, but he didn't look it. I had formerly estimated that he had been pudgy for about five years, but now I would have made it ten.

"It can't be done," I said. "With him a rule

is a rule. He's part mule. If it's really urgent he might talk on the phone."

"Get him."

"I'll try." I went to the kitchen, sat at the little table where I eat breakfast, reached for the house phone, and pushed the "P" button.

After a two-minute wait, about par, the usual "Yes?"

"Me in the kitchen. Amory Browning is in the office. I once saw a picture somewhere of a dragon snorting fire. That's him. He ordered me to get you down here now. I told him you might talk on the phone."

Silence for eight seconds, then: "Bring him."

"Okay, but have something ready to throw."

The elevator will take up to 600 pounds, but I thought a little deep breathing would be good for him, so I took him to the stairs, and he surprised me by not stopping to catch up on oxygen at the landings. He wasn't panting even at the top. As I said, he was behind me down the aisles, but when I opened the door to the potting room I let him by. Wolfe, in his long-sleeved, yellow smock, was at the side bench opening a bale of tree fern. He turned part way and said, "You don't like to be interrupted at work. Neither do I."

Browning was standing with his feet apart. "You goddam cheap bully!"

"Not 'cheap.' I haven't earned that reproach. What do you want?"

"Nothing. Calling my secretary a liar. Getting her here on a Saturday morning just to butter your ego by insulting her. I came to tell you that you can tell Mrs. Odell that there will be no more cooperation from anyone at CAN. Tell her if she wants to know why, to call me. Is that plain enough?"

"Yes indeed. Is that what you came for, to tell me that?"

"Yes!"

"Very well, you've told me." Wolfe turned back to the bale of tree fern.

Browning was stuck. Of course with the "Is that plain enough?" he should have whirled and headed for the door. Now what could he do for an exit? He could only just go, and I admit he had sense enough to realize it. He just went, and I followed, and again he didn't see an orchid. I supposed that on the way down the three flights he would decide on an exit line to use on me, but evidently he was too mad to bother, though I passed him down in the hall and opened the door for him. Not a word. I went to the office and sat to ask myself why I had bothered to deposit the check.

And in three minutes the doorbell rang and I went to the hall and there was Saul Panzer.

It's moments like that that make life worth living, seeing Saul there on the stoop. If he had just wanted to make a routine report or ask a question or ask for help, he would have phoned. If he had wanted to consult Wolfe, he would have waited until eleven o'clock. And if he had bad news, he would have let his face show it as I came down the hall. So he had something good. I opened the door wide and said, "My god, are you welcome. How good is it?"

"I guess I'm awful obvious," he said, and stepped in. "I *think* it's satisfactory."

I slammed the door shut. "For a nickel I'd kiss you." I looked at my wrist: 10:47. "You'd rather tell him, but I don't want to wait thirteen minutes. Neither do you or you wouldn't be here yet. We'll go up."

It took us about half as long as it had taken Browning and me. I won't say that we didn't see an orchid as we passed through the rooms, but we didn't stop to admire one. Wolfe, still in the yellow smock, was at the sink washing his hands, and Theodore stood there with a paper towel ready for him. Theodore babies him, which is one of the reasons he is not my favorite fellow being.

Wolfe, turning and seeing Saul, was on as quick as I had been. He said, "Indeed," and ignored the dripping water from his hands. "What?"

"Yes, sir," Saul said. "Once in a while I do something exactly right and am lucky along with it, and that's a pleasure. I would enjoy leading up to it, but it's been a long time since we've brought you anything. Dennis Copes's twin sister, Diana, is the wife of Lieutenant J. M. Rowcliff. They have two children, a boy and a girl. Dennis and Diana see each other quite often—as I said, twins."

Wolfe took the towel from Theodore, patted with it, dropped it in the bin, took another, rubbed with it, missed the bin. It fluttered to the floor and Theodore picked it up. Wolfe flattened his right palm against his left and made slow circles.

"Are Mr. Rowcliff and Mr. Copes on good terms?"

"No. They see each other very seldom. Apparently never would suit them fine."

"Mr. Rowcliff and his wife?"

"Three people say they're happy. I know it's hard to believe that anybody could stand Rowcliff, but off duty he may be different."

"Have you caused a stir?"

"No."

That was Saul. Not "I hope not" or "I don't think so." Just "No."

"More than satisfactory." Wolfe took the smock off and hung it on a wall hook, got his vest and jacket from a hanger, and put them on. He looked at the clock on the bench: two minutes to eleven. "I want a word with Theodore and I'll consider this on the way down. Put a bottle of champagne in the refrigerator, Archie—and Saul, we'll probably need you."

Saul and I went.

I suppose I shouldn't include what happened

next; it's just too pat. Who will believe it? But
Fred deserves to have it in, and it happened. Saul
and I had just got to the office, having stopped at
the kitchen on the way, and were discussing how
it should be handled, when the doorbell rang and
I went. It was Fred. I opened the door, and as he
entered he blurted, "Is he down yet?" I said he
was on the way and he said, "If I hold it in any
longer I'll bust. Copes's twin sister is married to
that sonofabitch Rowcliff."

All right, it happened. In nineteen days they
had got exactly nothing, and here came two of
them, practically simultaneous, with the same
beautiful slab of bacon. Saul, who had come to the
hall and heard him, said, "So we need *two* bottles
of champagne," and went to the kitchen. I was
telling Fred that Saul had beat him by just sixteen
minutes, when the elevator door opened and Wolfe
was there, and when he saw the look on Fred's
face, he knew what had happened, so I didn't have
to tell him, but I did. He led the way to the office,
and Saul came and he and Fred moved yellow
chairs up.

Wolfe sat and said, "Get Mr. Cramer."

He has been known to rush it, and it had been
a long dry spell. "You once made a remark," I said,
"about impetuosity. I could quote it verbatim."

"So could I. If we discussed it all day there
would still be only one way to learn if we have it
or not. Get him."

"If he's not there do you want Rowcliff?"

"No. Only Mr. Cramer."

I pulled the phone around and dialed, and got
first the switchboard, then a sergeant I knew only
by name, Molloy, and then Inspector Cramer, and
Wolfe took his phone. I stayed on.

Wolfe: "Good morning."

"Is it?"

"I think so. I have a problem. I must discuss
a matter with Mr. Rowcliff as soon as possible, and

it will go better if you are present. It relates to the death of Peter Odell. Could you come now?"

"No. I'll get Rowcliff on another phone."

"That wouldn't do. I have a tape recording both of you should hear."

"A recording of what?"

"You'll know when you hear it. You won't like it, but it may give you a useful hint. It has given me one."

"I can't—wait. Maybe I can. Hold it."

We held it for about two minutes, and then: "Does it have to be Rowcliff?"

"Yes. That's requisite."

"I never expected to hear this, you wanting to see Rowcliff. We'll leave in about ten minutes."

Click.

We hung up. I asked Wolfe, "The Copes tape?"

He said yes, and I went to the safe for the key to the locked cabinet where we keep various items that would be in the safe if there was room. Wolfe started in on Saul and Fred, asking questions that I thought should have been asked before calling Cramer, but he got nothing that tangled it. Fred had nothing but the bare fact that Copes's sister was Rowcliff's wife. Saul, knowing we would need more, had proceeded to get it, but he hadn't seen Diana herself, only neighbors and a woman who cleaned the Rowcliff apartment once a week, and two men who knew Copes. Almost certainly nothing had got to Rowcliff. However, one problem arose that had to be dealt with; Wolfe rang for beer and had the cap off of the bottle before he remembered that we were probably going to open champagne. He called Fritz in for consultation, and they decided it would be interesting to try eel stewed in stale beer, and Fritz thought he knew where he could get eel the next day. Wolfe told him Saul and Fred would join us for lunch, and it should be a little early if possible—one o'clock.

Lieutenant Rowcliff has it in for all private detectives, but I admit he has a special reason for thinking the world would be better off without me. When he gets hot he stutters, and with me it must be catching, because when he's working on me and I see that he is getting close to that point, *I* start to stutter, especially on words that begin with *g* or *t*. It's a misdemeanor to interfere with a police officer in the performance of his duty, but how could he handle that? Wolfe knows about it, and when the doorbell rang at a quarter to twelve and he told Saul to get it, I believe he actually thought I might greet them with "Gu-gu-gu-good morning."

I was at my desk. Fred was in one of the three yellow chairs facing Wolfe's desk, the one nearest me. Cramer, leading the way, of course went to the red leather chair, and Rowcliff took the yellow one nearest him, which left the middle one for Saul. As Cramer sat, he said, "Make it snappy. Rowcliff has someone waiting. What's this about a recording?"

"I'll have to introduce it," Wolfe said. "You probably know the name, Dennis Copes."

"I've heard it. One of the CAN bunch."

"I know him," Rowcliff said. "He wants Meer's job."

Wolfe nodded. "So it is said. As you know, Mrs. Odell's advertisement appeared last Tuesday, six days ago. Mr. Copes came here Thursday evening and said he had to admit something and that he had information to give me under the conditions stated in the advertisement. He did so. The recording is that conversation.—Archie?"

All I had to do was reach to the far corner of my desk to flip a switch. The playback, which was a honey and had cost $922.50, was on the desk at the back. We knew it was a good tape, since we had listened to it three times.

Copes's voice came. "That was a good ad. 'Any

person who communicates as a result of this advertisement thereby agrees to the above conditions.' Very neat. What agency?"

"Agency?"

"Who wrote it?"

"Mr. Goodwin."

Naturally I watched their faces. The first few minutes they looked at each other a couple of times, but then their eyes stayed mostly on Wolfe. Then Cramer set his jaw and his face got even redder than usual, and Rowcliff started to lick his lips. It has been said that Rowcliff is handsome, and I'll concede that his six feet of meat is distributed well enough, but his face reminds me of a camel with a built-in sneer. All right, I don't like him, so allow for it. Of course licking his lips didn't improve it any.

It got to the end. Wolfe: "You may have to. I can't tell you how I'll proceed, Mr. Copes, because I don't know. If I need you, I'll know where to find you." I reached to the switch and flipped it.

"By god," Cramer said. He was so mad his voice was weak. "Four days ago. Four whole days. And you even told him not to tell anybody anything. And *now* you get us here and— How in hell you expect—"

"Pfui," Wolfe said. "You're not a witling and you know I'm not. If I had believed he was telling the truth, I might or might not have informed you immediately, but I certainly would not have risked telling him not to. I had good reason to suspect that he wasn't. How could Kenneth Meer possibly have known that Odell intended to put LSD in the whisky? I don't know how much of an effort you have made to learn if anyone knew, and if so who, but I know how much *I* have. I thought it extremely doubtful that Meer could have known. But if he didn't, if Copes was lying, how did Copes know even now? Apparently it had been kept an official secret; it had not been disclosed by you or

the District Attorney. And I had to know. I had
to know if Copes could possibly have learned about
the LSD from any other source. Unless such a
source could be found, it would be impossible to
challenge his account, and I would have to advise
him to tell you without further delay. At ten
o'clock Friday morning, five of us gathered here to
consider it, and Mr. Panzer, Mr. Durkin, and Mr.
Cather were given instructions and proceeded to
inquire. The obvious possibil—"

"Three days you kept it. By God, three days
and three nights." Cramer's voice was not weak.

"The weekend intervened. Anyway I would
have kept it as long as there was any hope of find-
ing a probable source. Three weeks or three
months. Fortunately a competent performance by
Mr. Panzer—and Mr. Durkin—made it *only* three
days. Mr. Panzer brought it a little more than an
hour ago, and I telephoned you almost immediately. Copes lied. I know how he learned about the
LSD."

Wolfe looked at Rowcliff and back at Cramer.
"There are several ways I could do this, and I'm
taking the quickest, which should also be the most
effective. As you know, a friend of Mr. Goodwin's,
Mr. Cohen, is in a position of authority and influence at the *Gazette*." He turned. "Your notebook, Archie."

With no idea what was coming, I got it, and
a pen, and crossed my legs.

"A suggested draft for an article in tomorrow's *Gazette*. 'In an interview yesterday afternoon Nero Wolfe, comma, the private investigator,
comma, stated that an attempt has been made by
Dennis Copes, comma, an employee of the Continental Air Network, comma, to get the sixty-five
thousand dollars offered in a recent advertisement
by Mrs. Peter Odell, comma, by fraud. Period.'—
No. Instead of 'fraud' make it 'by subreption.' It's

more precise and will add to vocabularies. 'Paragraph.'

"'Mr. Wolfe said, comma, quote, "Dennis Copes came to my office last Thursday evening and disclosed that he had knowledge of a certain fact relevant to the explosion of a bomb in the office of a CAN executive on the twentieth of May that caused the death of Peter Odell. Period. It was a fact known to me and to the police but had never been divulged, comma, by them or by me. Period. It was a closely guarded secret. Period. Mr. Copes's explanation of how and where he had learned it made it highly probable that the bomb had been placed in the drawer by another employee of CAN, comma, named by him. Paragraph.

"'Quote. "I had reason to suspect that Mr. Copes's account of how he had learned the fact was false, comma, and I undertook to discover if he might have learned it some other way. Period. This morning I learned that there was indeed another way. Period. Mr. Copes has a twin sister named Diana who is the wife of a police lieutenant named J. M. Rowcliff. Period. I think it highly probable, comma, in fact I am satisfied, comma, that Mr. Rowcliff—"'"

"Why, goddamn you—" Rowcliff was up and moving.

"Back up!" Cramer snapped.

"Let me finish," Wolfe said.

"*I'll* finish you! You—"

"Can it!" Cramer snapped. "Sit down. Sit down and shut your trap." To Wolfe: "You know damn well you can't do this. We'd tear your guts out. You'd be done."

"I doubt it," Wolfe said. "The spotlight of public interest. I would be a cynosure, a man of mark. And my client's resources are considerable. I would have handled this differently if it were not Mr. Rowcliff. If it were Mr. Stebbins, for instance,

I would have asked him to come and I would have told him that I wanted merely his private acknowledgment that he had told his wife about the LSD. That would have satisfied *me* that Mr. Copes had learned of the LSD from his sister, and no further proof would have been required. It would not have been necessary even for you to be told, either by him or by me. But with Mr. Rowcliff that would not have been possible. Would it? You know him. You know his animus against me."

"You could have asked *me* to come. And discuss it."

"Certainly. I have. Here we are."

"Balls. Discuss, my ass. 'In an interview yesterday afternoon Nero Wolfe, the private investigator.' That crap. All right, I'll discuss it with Rowcliff and you'll hear from me later. Probably today."

"No." Emphatic. "That won't do. It's urgent. There's a certain step I intend to take without delay. I'll postpone it only if I must. If you and Mr. Rowcliff leave without satisfying me, Mr. Goodwin will leave ten minutes later with the suggested draft for that article. It may be possible to get it in the late edition of today's paper. And of course reporters will be wanting to see Mr. and Mrs. Rowcliff—and you, I suppose. This is probably a resort to coercion, but I make no apology; the fact that I have Mr. Rowcliff to deal with makes it imperative. Actually I don't ask much. I require only a statement by him, unequivocal, that he told his wife about the LSD found in Peter Odell's pocket. I don't need an admission by his wife that she told her brother. That is a plausible assumption that for me will suffice."

Wolfe turned to Rowcliff. "You may know—or you may not—that there is an understanding between Mr. Cramer and me which he knows I observe. No conversation in this office with him present is recorded without his express consent. This is not being recorded."

"You goddamn ape," Rowcliff said.

Cramer asked him, "Did you hear me tell you to shut your trap?"

No reply.

"Say 'yes, sir,' " Cramer said.

Rowcliff licked his lips. "Yes, sir."

"You're a good cop," Cramer said. "I know what you're good for and what you're not good for. I even agree with your opinion of Wolfe up to a point, but *only* up to a point. That understanding he mentioned, you wouldn't trust him to keep it, but I do. That's a flaw you've got. Anyway the point right now is not our opinion of Wolfe, it's what he wants from you. There are aspects of this that you and I can discuss privately, and we will, but if you *did* tell your wife about the LSD, and you can be damn sure I'm going to *know* if you did, the best thing you can do is to say so here and now. You don't have to tell Wolfe, tell me. Did you?"

"Goddam it, Inspector, I'm not—"

"Did you?"

"Yes. I'm not going—"

"Shut up." Cramer turned to Wolfe. "I call that unequivocal, damn you."

"So do I," Wolfe said. "Thank you for coming."

"You can shove your thanks." He stood up. "You said something on the phone about a useful hint. You can shove that too. You and your useful hints." He turned to Rowcliff. "You, move. Move!"

It was an order and Rowcliff obeyed it. Anyone else I could name, I would have felt sorry for him. I knew what he had coming and so did he. Saul followed them to the hall; he had let them in, so he would check them out.

As Saul came back in, Wolfe told me, "Get Mr. Browning."

He was certainly making up for lost time, but it had worked with Cramer and Rowcliff so it might work with the next president of CAN too, whatever it was. I pulled the phone around and dialed, and told the switchboard I wanted to speak to Mr. Browning's secretary. When you ask for secretaries usually you aren't asked who you are, and in a minute I had her.

"Mr. Browning's office."

"Miss Lugos, please."

"This is Miss Lugos."

"This is Archie Goodwin. Mr. Wolfe would like to speak to Mr. Browning."

"Nero Wolfe?"

"Yes."

"What about?"

"I don't know. It must be important, since Mr. Browning called him a cheap bully only a couple of hours ago."

"I'll see. Hold the wire."

Of course she would tell me either that Mr. Browning was not available or to put Mr. Wolfe on. But she didn't. After a wait of only a couple of minutes, his voice: "What do you want?"

I didn't have to answer because Wolfe was on.

"Mr. Browning?"

"Yes."

"Nero Wolfe. I have just spoken at some length with Inspector Cramer of the police. He left my office five minutes ago. This afternoon, not later than four o'clock, I am going to tell him who put a bomb in a drawer of your desk, and I think it fitting and desirable that I tell you first. I would also like to tell Miss Lugos why I told her that she lied. Will you come, with her, at half past two?"

Silence, a long minute, then, "I think *you're* lying."

"No. A lie that would be exposed in three hours? No."

"You know who did that? You know now?"

"Yes."

A shorter silence. "I'll call you back."

He hung up. Of course that meant yes. He wouldn't call Cramer, and even if he did, what would that get him? I looked at Wolfe. Sometimes you can tell pretty well how good his hand is by the way he holds his head, and his mouth. That time I couldn't. No sign. I asked him, "Must we leave the room while you're telling them? We're curious. We'd like to know too."

"You will." He looked at the wall clock. 12:25. "Now. Saul, ask Fritz to bring the champagne."

As Saul left, the doorbell rang, and I went. It was Orrie Cather. I opened the door and said, "Greetings. Go ahead and tell me you know who Dennis Copes's twin sister's husband is."

"Huh?" He stepped in. "I didn't know he had a sister. I got bounced from the CAN building."

"Sure. They knew you like champagne. Go right in."

So Orrie was there for the briefing too.

19

*t*he vice-president and his secretary came on the dot at half past two. Precisely.

We were well-filled. Inside our bellies were three bottles of Dom Perignon champagne, braised sweetbreads with chicken quenelles (small portions because of the unexpected guests), crab meat omelets (added attraction), celery and mushroom salad, and four kinds of cheese. Inside our skulls were the details of where it stood according to Wolfe and the program for the next hour or two. For where it stood I would have given good odds, say ten to one, and so would the other three. For the program, no bet. It was a typical Wolfe concoction. It assumed—*he* assumed—that if an unexpected snag interfered, he would be able to handle it no matter what it was, and your ego has to be riding high to assume that.

To prepare for it only two props were needed. One was the Copes tape in the playback on my desk. For the other all four of us went to the basement. I could have done it alone, but they wanted to help. In a corner of the big storage room there were two thick, old mattresses, no springs in them, which I had used a few times for targets to get bullets for comparison purposes. We decided the best place for them was under the pool table in the adjoining room, where it had been installed when Wolfe had decided that he needed some violent exercise. Doubled, the mattresses were a tight fit under it.

The three were to be in the front room, but when the doorbell rang Saul went to receive the guests and show them in. They didn't have their war paint on. Browning was not a dragon snorting fire, and Helen Lugos was not set to use her claws on someone who had called her a liar. He sat in the red leather chair and said he had an appointment at a quarter past three, and she sat in a yellow one and said nothing.

"This will take a while," Wolfe told Browning. "Perhaps an hour."

"I can't stay an hour."

"We'll see. I'll make it as brief as possible. First you must hear a recording of a conversation I had recently with a member of your staff, Dennis Copes. Here. He came last Thursday evening.— Archie?"

I flipped the switch, and for the fifth time I heard Copes speak highly of that ad. Another time or two and I would begin to think I had picked the wrong line of work, that by now I could have been a vice-president myself, at one of the big agencies. As I had with Cramer and Rowcliff, I watched their faces. Their reaction was very different from the cops'. They looked at Wolfe hardly at all. Mostly they looked at each other, him with a frown that developed into what you might call a gawk, and her first with her eyes wide and then with her lips parted. Twice she started to say something but realized she had to hold it. When it came to the end and I turned it off, they both started to speak at once, he to her and she to him, but Wolfe stopped them. "Don't," he said, loud enough and decisive enough to stop anybody. "Don't waste your breath and your time and mine, I know he lied. It was all a fabrication. That has been established, with the help of Inspector Cramer. He heard the recording this morning. I should tell you, and I do, that this conversation is not being recorded. I give you that assurance on my word of honor, and those who know me would tell you that I would not tarnish that fine old pledge."

Browning demanded, "If you know he lied why bother us with it? Why do *you* waste our time?"

"I don't. You *had* to hear part of it, and to appreciate that part you needed to hear the whole. I have—"

"What part?"

"You said your time is limited."

"It is."

"Then don't interrupt. I have a good deal to say and I am not garrulous. The kernel of Mr. Copes's fabrication was of course the quotation—what he said he heard Kenneth Meer say." To Helen Lugos: "You say he didn't say that? That that conversation didn't occur?"

"I certainly do. It didn't."

"I believe you. But his invention of it told me something that he did not intend and was not aware of. It told me who put the bomb in the drawer, and I'm going to tell you how and why. As I said, I'll make it brief as possible, but you should know that Kenneth Meer is responsible for my concern in this affair. On May twenty-sixth, a Monday, he went to a clinic, gave a false name, and told a doctor that he needed help; that he got blood on his hands recurrently, frequently, not visible to anyone else. He refused—"

Browning demanded, "A clinic? What clinic?"

"Don't interrupt! To include all details would take all day. I assure you that anything I do include can be verified. He refused to give any information about himself. A friend of that doctor, another doctor, consulted me, and Kenneth Meer, still using an alias, came to see me. He still refused to supply any information about himself, but by a ruse, Mr. Goodwin and I learned who he was, and of course we had seen his name in the published reports of the death of Peter Odell. That led to my being consulted by Mrs. Odell and her hiring me. Naturally—"

"So that's how—"

"Don't interrupt! Naturally I considered the possibility that Meer had supplied the bomb and was racked by his sense of guilt. But surely not intending it for you, and information given me by Mrs. Odell made it extremely unlikely that he could have known that Peter Odell intended to go to your room and open that drawer. I will not elaborate on that. I have included that detail, how I first saw Kenneth Meer, only to explain why he has been of special interest throughout. There has always been for me that special reason to suspect him, but there was no plausible basis for a charge. Or rather, there was, but I hadn't the wit to see it. I admit I should have. Mr. Copes revealed it to me."

He turned a palm up. "If you undertake to invent something you heard another man say and you're not a fool, you make it conform to his character, his knowledge, and his style. And Copes had Kenneth Meer saying to Miss Lugos, 'I want to be damn sure you don't open the drawer to take a look at the usual time.' Would he have had him say that to her, especially the 'usual time,' unless he knew, or thought he knew, that Miss Lugos was in the habit of looking in the drawer every day, and that Meer knew it? When he wanted to make the invented quotation not only conceivable but as credible as possible? He would not. He would have included that 'usual' only if it conformed to his knowledge of the facts. Of course if he knew that Miss Lugos had told the police—and Mr. Goodwin —that she had *not* habitually opened the drawer every day, it was a blunder to include the 'usual.' It was a blunder even if he didn't know that, because it wasn't necessary, but he included it because he thought it increased the credibility of his lie."

Wolfe looked at Helen Lugos. "So when you told Mr. Goodwin that you did not look in the drawer every day, *you* lied. And you knew that the bomb, put in the drawer by Kenneth Meer, was intended for *you*. You had known that from the day it happened. You probably knew it, at least surmised it, the moment you entered the wrecked room."

Browning was on his feet. "Come, Helen," he said. "This is absurd. We're going."

"No," Wolfe said. He turned to me, lifted a hand, and wiggled a finger. I went and opened the connecting door to the front room and stuck my head in and said, "Help." Saul and Fred headed for the other door, to the hall, and Orrie came and joined me. Helen Lugos was up and moving, with Browning behind her, but before they reached the door to the hall Saul and Fred were there, and Helen Lugos stopped. Saul swung the door around, closed it, and he and Fred stood with their backs to it.

"You are *not* going, Mr. Browning," Wolfe said. "Come and sit down."

Browning turned. "This *is* absurd. Absolutely ridiculous."

"It is not. I have more to say and I mean you to hear it. You might as well sit."

"No. You'll regret this."

"I doubt it." Wolfe turned. "Your notebook, Archie."

I went to my desk, sat, got notebook and pen, and crossed my legs. A replay, though not quite instant.

Wolfe leaned back. "A suggested draft for an article in tomorrow's *Gazette*. 'Yesterday afternoon Nero Wolfe, comma, the private investigator, comma, told a *Gazette* reporter that he has learned who was responsible for the death by violence of Peter Odell, comma, a vice-president of the Continental Air Network, comma, on May twentieth. Period. Mr. Odell was killed by the explosion of a bomb in the office of Amory Browning, comma, also a vice-president of the Continental Air Network. Paragraph.

" 'Mr. Wolfe said, comma, quote, "I have established to my satisfaction that the bomb was put in a drawer of Mr. Browning's desk by Kenneth Meer, comma, Mr. Browning's assistant, dash, the drawer in which Mr. Browning kept a supply of bourbon whisky. Period. Mr. Meer knew that Miss Helen Lugos, comma, Mr. Browning's secretary, comma, was in the habit of opening the drawer every afternoon to see that the whisky was there, comma, and he placed the bomb so it would explode when the drawer was opened. Period. However, comma, Mr. Odell entered the room shortly after three o'clock and opened the drawer, comma, it is not known why. Paragraph.

" 'Quote. "In these circumstances, comma, established to my satisfaction, comma, it is not only reasonable, comma, it is unavoidable, comma, to suppose that Miss Lugos has been aware that the bomb must have been put in the drawer by Mr. Meer, comma, and the supposition is supported by the fact that she has consistently denied that she habitually opened the drawer every day to check on the whisky. Period. Also it is reasonable to suppose that Mr. Browning was aware of that too, comma, or at least suspected it. Period. Kenneth Meer knew of the intimate personal relationship that existed between Mr. Browning and Miss Lugos, comma, and was tormented by the knowledge. Period. He was torn by two intense and conflicting desires. Colon. His ardent wish to advance through his association with Mr. Browning, comma, and his concupiscence. Period. It may be assumed—" ' "

"This is worse than ridiculous." Browning was standing at the end of Wolfe's desk. "It's idiotic. No newspaper would print it. Any of it."

"Oh, yes. The *Gazette* would, with a guaranty from Mrs. Odell to cover all expenses. Yes, indeed. You're up a stump, Mr. Browning, and so is Miss Lugos. Not only the publicity; you would have to sue for libel, or persuade the District Attorney to charge us with criminal libel. That would be obligatory, and both of you would have to submit to questioning under oath. *That* would be idiotic, for a man in your position."

For the second time that day something happened that was hard to believe. Browning stood with his eyes glued to Wolfe, but probably not really seeing him, his shoulders set, and his chin back. Twenty seconds, half a minute, I don't know; and then he turned right around and looked at Helen Lugos, who had stayed over by the door, an arm's reach from Saul and Orrie. And she said, "Ask him what he wants." It was a suggestion, not a command, but even so, from a secretary to a vice-president soon to be a president? Women's Lib, or what?

Whatever it was, it worked fine. He turned back to Wolfe and asked, "What do you want?"

"I like eyes at a level," Wolfe said. "Please sit down."

Helen Lugos came back to the yellow chair, and sat. At least she left the red leather chair for him, and he took it, or some of it—about the front eight inches of the seat, barely enough to keep his rump on—and asked again, "What do you want?"

"From you, not much," Wolfe said. "I am not Jupiter Fidius. I want only to do the job I was hired to do. I think I know the present state of Kenneth Meer's mind. His mood, his spirit. I think he's pregnable. I want to get him on the telephone, tell him you and Miss Lugos are here, and ask him to join us for a discussion. If he refuses or demurs, I want you to speak to him and tell him to come. I don't know how things stand between you and him; of course during these six weeks you would have liked to turn him out, but didn't dare. Will he come if you tell him to?"

"Yes. Then what?"

"We'll see. One possibility, he may acknowledge that he put the bomb in the drawer, but claim that it was intended for Peter Odell—that he knew that Odell intended to come and open the drawer. There are other possibilities, and it may be that his real motive need not be divulged. That would please you and Miss Lugos, and I have no animus against you, but I make no commitment. This is your one chance to get out of it with minor bruises. I know too much now that the police *should* know."

Would he ask her for another suggestion? No. He looked at her, but only for a second, and then said, "All right. If you think—all right."

Wolfe turned to me: "Get him."

That was one of the possible snags. What if he wasn't there? What if he had got a toothache or twisted an ankle and left for the day? But he hadn't. I got him and Wolfe got on. I stayed on.

"Good afternoon, Mr. Meer. I'm calling from my office, at the suggestion of Mr. Browning. He and Miss Lugos are here. We have talked at some length, and have come to a point where we need your help. Can you come at once?"

"Why—they're there?"

"Yes. Since half past two."

"Mr. Browning told you to call me?"

"Yes. He's right here. Do you want to speak to him?"

"I don't—no. No. All right. I'll leave in five minutes."

He hung up. Wolfe told Browning, "He'll leave in five minutes. You and Miss Lugos may wish to speak privately. This room is sound-proofed." He stood. "Would you like something to drink?"

Browning looked at her and she shook her head, and he said, "No." Saul and Fred left by the hall door, closing it after them, and Wolfe and Orrie and I left by the door to the front room. In a moment Saul and Fred joined us. Wolfe said, "I'm going to the kitchen. I'm thirsty. Any questions? Any comments?"

Orrie said, "It's all set. It's up to him."

Wolfe went by the hall door. Fred said, "If anyone wants a bet, I'm giving two to one that he'll have it."

Saul said, "I'd rather have your end."

I said, "I don't want *either* end."

They debated it. At a time like that, it only makes it longer to keep looking at your watch, but that's what I did. 3:22, 3:24, 3:27. At that time of day there should be taxis headed downtown on Ninth Avenue in the Fifties, and it was only nineteen blocks. At half past three I went to the hall, leaving the door open, and stood with my nose against the one-way glass of the front door. Me and my watch. 3:32, 3:34, 3:36. He had been run over by a truck or something. He was on his way to the airport. At 3:37 a taxi rolled up in front and stopped alongside the parked cars, and the door opened, and he climbed out, and he had the brief case. I called through the open door to the front room, "Okay, he has it!" and they came. Orrie went down the hall to the door to the office and stood. Fred stood at my left by the rack; he would be behind the door when I opened it. Saul stood in the doorway to the front room. Kenneth Meer mounted the stoop with the brief case tucked under his left arm. He pushed the button, and I counted a slow ten and opened the door, and he stepped in. With the brief case under his arm, that hand was pressed against his left hip, and his

right hand was hanging loose. I don't think I have
ever made a faster or surer move. Facing him, I
got his two wrists, and I got them good, and Saul,
from behind him, got the brief case. His mouth
popped open but no sound came, and he went stiff
top to bottom, absolutely stiff. Then he tried to
turn around, but I had his wrists, and only his
head could turn. Saul had backed away, holding
the brief case against his belly with both hands.
I said, "Go ahead and don't drop it," and he
started down the hall to the rear, where the stair
to the basement was, and at the door to the office
Orrie joined him. I let go of Meer's wrists, and he
stood, still stiff, and stared down the hall at Saul
going. He still hadn't made a sound. Then suddenly
he started to slump. He made it over to the bench,
flopped down on it, bent over with his face in his
hands, and started to shake all over. Still no sound,
absolutely none. I told Fred, "Keep him company,"
and headed for the kitchen.

Wolfe was on his stool at the center table with
a beer glass in his hand. "You win," I said. "He
had it and we got it."

"Where is he?"

"In the hall."

You wouldn't believe how easy and smooth
he can remove his seventh of a ton off of a stool.
I followed him down the hall. Meer was still
huddled on the bench and still shaking. Wolfe
stood and looked down at him for a good ten
seconds, told Fred, "Stay here," went back down
the hall and opened the office door and entered, and
I followed. Browning, in the red leather chair,
asked, "Did he come? The doorbell rang five
min—"

"Shut up," Wolfe snapped, and crossed to his
desk and sat and glared at them. "Yes," he said,
"he came. When he came Saturday, day before
yesterday, he was in his own car, but he didn't
leave his brief case in it. He kept it with him, and

167

he kept it in his lap as he sat where you are now. When I decided today to ask him to come, later, I thought it likely that he would bring the brief case, and if so there would be a bomb in it, since he would know you two were here. It was only a conjecture, but well-grounded, and it has been verified. He came, and he had the brief case, and it is now in my basement under a pile of mattresses. On your way out, you will pass him in the hall—prostrated, wretched, defeated. Pass him, just pass him. He is no longer yours. I am now—"

"But my god, what—"

"*Shut up!* I am now going to call Mr. Cramer and ask him to come and bring with him men who know how to deal with bombs. If you don't want to encounter him, leave at once. Go."

He turned to me. "Get him, Archie."

I swiveled and dialed.

ABOUT THE AUTHOR

REX STOUT, the creator of Nero Wolfe, was born in Noblesville, Indiana, in 1886, the sixth of nine children of John and Lucetta Todhunter Stout, both Quakers. Shortly after his birth, the family moved to Wakarusa, Kansas. He was educated in a country school, but, by the age of nine, was recognized throughout the state as a prodigy in arithmetic. Mr. Stout briefly attended the University of Kansas, but left to enlist in the Navy, and spent the next two years as a warrant officer on board President Theodore Roosevelt's yacht. When he left the Navy in 1908, Rex Stout began to write freelance articles, worked as a sightseeing guide and as an itinerant bookkeeper. Later he devised and implemented a school banking system which was installed in four hundred cities and towns throughout the country. In 1927 Mr. Stout retired from the world of finance and, with the proceeds of his banking scheme, left for Paris to write serious fiction. He wrote three novels that received favorable reviews before turning to detective fiction. His first Nero Wolfe novel, *Fer-de-Lance*, appeared in 1934. It was followed by many others, among them, *Too Many Cooks, The Silent Speaker, If Death Ever Slept, The Doorbell Rang* and *Please Pass the Guilt*, which established Nero Wolfe as a leading character on a par with Erle Stanley Gardner's famous protagonist, Perry Mason. During World War II, Rex Stout waged a personal campaign against Nazism as chairman of the War Writers' Board, master of ceremonies of the radio program "Speaking of Liberty" and as a member of several national committees. After the war, he turned his attention to mobilizing public opinion against the wartime use of thermo-nuclear devices, was an active leader in the Authors' Guild and resumed writing his Nero Wolfe novels. All together, his Nero Wolfe novels have been translated into twenty-two languages and have sold more than forty-five million copies. Rex Stout died in 1975 at the age of eighty-eight. A month before his death, he published his forty-sixth Nero Wolfe novel, *A Family Affair*.

THE MYSTERIOUS WORLD OF AGATHA CHRISTIE

Acknowledged as the world's most popular mystery writer of all time, Dame Agatha Christie's books have thrilled millions of readers for generations. With her care and attention to characters, the intriguing situations and the breathtaking final deduction, it's no wonder that Agatha Christie is the world's best selling mystery writer.

WHODUNIT?

Bantam did! By bringing you these masterful tales of murder, suspense and mystery!

☐	10706	**SLEEPING MURDER** by Agatha Christie	$2.25
☐	11915	**THE MYSTERIOUS AFFAIR AT STYLES** by Agatha Christie	$1.95
☐	11922	**DEATH ON THE NILE** by Agatha Christie	$1.95
☐	12247	**THE SECRET ADVERSARY** by Agatha Christie	$1.95
☐	11926	**POIROT INVESTIGATES** by Agatha Christie	$1.95
☐	12078	**POSTERN OF FATE** by Agatha Christie	$1.95
☐	12355	**THE SPY WHO CAME IN FROM THE COLD** by John LeCarre	$2.50
☐	10910	**THE DROWNING POOL** by Ross Macdonald	$1.75
☐	11240	**THE UNDERGROUND MAN** by Ross Macdonald	$1.75

Bantam Book Catalog

Here's your up-to-the-minute listing of over 1,400 titles by your favorite authors.

This illustrated, large format catalog gives a description of each title. For your convenience, it is divided into categories in fiction and non-fiction—gothics, science fiction, westerns, mysteries, cookbooks, mysticism and occult, biographies, history, family living, health, psychology, art.

So don't delay—take advantage of this special opportunity to increase your reading pleasure.

Just send us your name and address and 50¢ (to help defray postage and handling costs).

BANTAM BOOKS, INC.
Dept. FC, 414 East Golf Road, Des Plaines, Ill. 60016

Mr./Mrs./Miss_____
(please print)

Address_____

City_____ State_____ Zip_____

Do you know someone who enjoys books? Just give us their names and addresses and we'll send them a catalog too!

_____

Mr./Mrs./Miss_____

Address_____

City_____ State_____ Zip_____

_____

Mr./Mrs./Miss_____

Address_____

City_____ State_____ Zip_____

FC—9/78